BRENIN

SAVAGE DRAGONS BOOK 4

KATHI S. BARTON

World Castle Publishing, LLC
Pensacola, Florida

Hardback ISBN: 9798249618773
Paperback ISBN: 9798891265349
eBook ISBN: 9798891265356
First Edition World Castle Publishing, LLC, April 20, 2026
http://www.worldcastlepublishing.com

Licensing Notes

Cover: Cover Designs by Karen
Editor: Karen Fuller

Chapter 1

"How are the checks made out? To Tank and Ace like we wanted them to be?" Cassian told his brother that they were and that he was excited to give them to the other two. "I am as well. It'll be nice for the money to go to something good rather than gather dust, not being cashed by either one of us."

He and Cassian were brothers, and their parents had both been condemned to death by the dragon council. Even their sister Margo, a mean bitch if there ever was one, had also been killed when the council had decided that they'd done enough misdeeds in the world and it was time to take them to task. There were insurance policies taken out on them before they died, and it was left to the two of them as their only living relatives. Neither one of them wanted the money, as it had been tainted because it had belonged to them.

They were giving the insurance checks to their cousins, Ace and Tank, to use as they saw fit. They had no use for the money in the first place and thought that their cousins, who were down on their luck, could use it more. They'd only been around for about a hundred years and had yet been able to save money like they had. He just hoped that they'd take it and use it for good.

"How did you want to give it to them? I mean, just say here and be done with it?" He said that he thought that they could do better than that. "I guess so. I've never been this excited about giving someone millions of dollars before. Am I getting so jaded that I would rather give it away than figure out something else to use it for?"

Brenin laughed. "It could be that. I know that I'm excited to be giving it to them, too. But we'll have to explain why we don't want the money. They might even be able to guess, but I don't want them to turn us down, so we can't just shove it at them and hope they take it." Cassian said he supposed not. "We have to be delicate with money like this. It's well over five million dollars, and we really want them to take it."

"Well, I hope you're ready because they just pulled into the driveway to visit us. Do you have this delicate way for them to take it practiced?" He said he'd not given it any thought. "Well, then we go with plan B and tell them they have to take it because we said so." They were both laughing when they joined them in Cassian's living room.

After hugs were given, the best part of greeting his cousins; they invited them to have a seat. Brenin was leaving the giving part up to his brother, and when he sat down, waiting expectantly for his brother to speak, he just pulled out the two checks and shoved them at them.

"Here. We don't want this, so we're giving it to you." Then he sat down too. Rolling his eyes, Brenin got up and tried to explain. But Cassian cut him off. "It was from our parents and Margo. You might as well take it because we don't want it."

"This is a lot of money to be just giving away." Of course, Ace would be worried about the amount instead of just taking the money from them. "I mean, I'm not saying that we can't use it, but really, it's a lot of money."

"Our parents must have taken it out when they were younger or something. Margo would have gotten it, I'm sure, as they wouldn't want us to have it. But since we did get it, we want you two to have it." He looked around the room. "That made no sense whatsoever. I'm sorry. I'm not doing this very well. Our parents took out these policies, and so did Margo. Or Mom and Dad took it out on her, we'll never know. But the money came to us as their only living relatives, and we have no use for it. The first people we thought of to give it away were the two of you. Tell us you'll take it from us so we don't have to worry with it anymore."

"The checks are already made out to us. I mean, you really meant for us to have this money." Brenin said, of course, they had. "I'm sorry. This is a lot to take in. We came over to see if you wanted to have lunch with us. This is quite a surprise."

"Yes, we'd love to have lunch with you. Raven is working with Skye and Kaida today, so it would have been just us anyway." Standing up after only just sitting down, he grabbed his coat and headed to the door with the rest of them. "The bank will give you grief about cashing the check, but we'll take care of him. He's been our banker for the past twenty or so years, and I'll talk to him about it."

There was some confusion about where they were going, but it got settled out in the end. Cassian suggested they go to the diner on the other end of town, and that was all right with the other two. As soon as they were seated, the checks having been put away for now, they talked about Ace's job as mayor. Tank was his assistant in the deal, and they were doing such a good job at their jobs that he doubted anyone would ever want to vote them out of office again.

"I've found more money in the way of grants to use in the town proper. It's for new lights that would light up the main street. They're going to be put in once winter is over, and they'll be perfect for hanging all the lights on for the holidays. It seems like they just put them away, and now we're about ready to have them put back out." Cassian said that they were all broken from being out for so long when they noticed them. "I can't get decorations with the money, but the lights will be nice to light up Main Street when the kids are out walking around at Halloween over the next few years."

"That's wonderful news. You've saved the taxpayers so much money this year, and you've only been in office all of six months, right?" He said it was about that. "I went by the pool the other day, and it's beginning to look good. They said that the foundation would be done by the end of September, and that's about four weeks away. Then there are the bathrooms that are going to be put in as well. It's looking really good."

"We've only run into one snag, and that was when they were going to put the lift in for the handicapped. It wasn't that big of a deal, but we had to enlarge the area around the lift so that the person using it would have enough room to get on it and off it without any trouble." He told Ace that it was coming along nicely. "I'll say. I was out there just this morning, and I can't believe how much better it's looking. With the larger pool, we're going to be able to have more people swimming than before. Not to mention the memberships that are selling. A lot of people want to use a portion of it to have birthday parties there. And the lifeguards are going to be a big hit with the younger parents. I have twenty-three applicants who want to have their lifeguard training to be paid for, and they'll work for us throughout the summer months until it's paid off. We'll still pay them, but this is working out better than we could have hoped it would."

"I'm so happy that you ran for the Mayoral position. The town is really starting to look like someone is around that cares." He thanked them and blushed slightly. "What are you going to do when there is no more help needed around town? But then I'm sure that there will be something that needs your attention."

"I hope so. I'm having fun. And making so many new friends. We never had any friends all that much where we lived before. This is an unexpected bonus of being mayor." He asked about their old house. "This money will help. We've been making payments on it since we moved here, and it's been difficult. We still have the PI business that we own, but it's not getting as much business as we thought it might. I don't know how much longer we're going to be doing that."

"That's a shame. I know you were really good at it." They had magic that would allow them to find someone right away if they had some kind of connection to them. Be it just a shirt or something that used to belong to them, they could find them. When they'd first met them, that was the way they were supporting themselves. He wondered what had happened that made it so they didn't want to do it anymore. He wondered if it had just been something that the two of them were doing before they got the mayoral position.

After lunch, they went to the bank with them so that they'd have no trouble with the checks. They'd had the insurance people divide the checks into two equal parts so that they'd both have money. The banker had been prepared for them, so they had no trouble at all with them. He was glad, but he was still afraid that they'd change their mind about taking them if there had been too much in the way of trouble.

Going back to his house, he had plenty to do; he started working on the paperwork that he'd left behind in favor of getting the checks to his cousins. Glad now that they'd done it that way, Ace and Tank both were so grateful that they both cried when the checks were deposited into their accounts; they must have thanked them about twenty times each for thinking of them. It was his pleasure not to have anything to do with the ill-gotten gains from his parents and sister. Cassian felt the same way about the money, and they were glad that someone would put it to good use.

By the time he was hungry again, he decided that dinner at home would be good. He had his cook make him a sub sandwich, and he had it with a baked potato.

After getting his fill, Brenin sat in the living room with the television on, reading a book. The game on the set wasn't as interesting as the book he was reading, and he was all right with that. Sometimes reading was by far more fun than doing anything else that was going on around the house.

Going up to bed after finishing the book, he was surprised that he'd enjoyed it that much. Tomorrow, he'd write a review on the book; he'd heard how authors really enjoyed getting feedback on their work, and he seldom read something without giving it a review. He'd do his best to get it done quickly because he didn't want to forget. As he was getting into bed, he thought of Ace and Tank.

Ace had been able to get all kinds of grants of money to help out around town. There had even been money for the lift being put into the pool for people to use. Then there was the money that he'd found for small business owners that took care of their broken windows along Main Street when their businesses had collapsed. He was a wizard at finding money for others to use as well as the town. It was making things like sidewalks along the main streets to be repaired for little to no money from taxes being raised.

Tank was a great assistant, too, in that he would scope out things that they'd been told about that needed to be improved. Twice now, things were worse than they thought, and it had to be taken care of right away. But all in all, the town was looking better than it had before, and everyone loved it. They loved the two men, too, and that was wonderful.

Brenin was going to be out of town for the next several days and put his phone on the service when he was ready to go. Calling his brother, he reminded him that he'd be out of town and also reminded him to get his mail. He could have had it stopped, but since he was going to be gone for only a few days, it was easier just to have Cassian pick it up for him. There was usually nothing more than advertisements and credit card offers anyway.

He was going to be looking at a business that was thinking about coming to town to bring jobs to the area. He was going there to see how they would fit in the community. And whether or not they'd have enough people to work the jobs that the business would create. It would be a total waste of time and money if they were to be too large for their area and not be able to get enough employees to work the shifts. There were a lot of people out of work, but if they wanted more than they could handle, it would be a flop.

Brenin had another date tonight. He'd been enjoying himself dating other shifters because they knew that there would be nothing long-term between them. Sometimes they got together just for sex, but most of the time they would go to dinner and see a movie. It was fun, and they would part as friends.

Picking Dana up at six, the two of them had a nice dinner. They were trying a new place in Zanesville that specialized in Mexican food. They enjoyed a good appetizer and then dinner. When it came to having dessert, they both declined in favor of getting an ice cream at Tom's Ice Cream Bowl, still in the town. They had the best cherry ice cream in the state as far as he was concerned, and Dana got herself a chocolate malt. As they were leaving, she said that she had a pounding headache and wanted to go home. He took her straight home and walked her to the door.

"Are you going to be all right?" She said that she'd be all right, as she got them once in a while. "Well, don't suffer needlessly. If you have something to take for it, then do it. No one would want you coming to work if you feel that bad."

"You're a nice man, Brenin. Why haven't you found your mate yet? She'd be lucky to have you in her life." He said that he was looking, but she wasn't his mate. "Good one. I'll see you around. Try to find her before she gets married to someone else, then you'll have a problem."

He knew that the same thing had happened to Dana's brother Carl. He'd been looking for his mate only to find out that she'd been married to another man for years, and she wasn't willing to give up on a sure thing. He'd ended up killing himself over it, and she'd never been the same since. His heart broke for the other woman, and he wondered if she had someone out there for herself. He hoped so. She was a wonderful person, too.

~*~

Lisa was on her last table when she got a phone call from the school. Nervous about getting a call from anyone at work, she took the call and waited for them to put her on hold. Who did that sort of thing? Call a person about an emergency only to be put on hold so that she could talk to them.

"Mrs. Manchester? There's been an accident at the school. Your son is all right, but he's very upset that his other friend Toby is hurt." She asked what had happened. "There was an incident on the play yard, and he was hurt by a bigger boy. He's going to be fine as well, just needs a few stitches, but it's your son who is upset the most. He said his best friend in the whole wide world is hurt, and he can't help him. I knew your son was tender-hearted, but this about broke all of our hearts. He wants to go home with him so he can take care of him."

"That's terrible news about Toby." Again, she was upset about how much information the school and daycare that Davy went to gave out information so freely. "Does he want me to come and get him? I can, it's no problem here."

"I think he just needs to talk to you. He is pretty upset." She told the woman that she'd be more than happy to come and get him. "That might be the best thing. He's still crying, and I'm fearful that he's going to make himself sick over this."

"I'll leave here in a few minutes. Tell him that I'm coming." She said that she'd do that and hung up the phone. Leaving her last table would be hard, but something that she'd done before when her son got sick. Davy might only be seven, but he was big hearted when it came to others that he considered friends. She told her boss what was going on, and they told her to leave. She was there to get him twenty minutes later and was glad that she'd gone to get him.

He was inconsolable. After taking him home, glad that she didn't have to work tonight, he laid down on his bed and cried himself to sleep. He kept going on about the bully not hitting him, but hitting his friend. She had a feeling that Toby had saved her son from a good beating by stepping in, and it hurt her that there were still bullies around the school. When he finally fell asleep, she closed his door and worked on grading papers for the local high school until he got up.

Just as she thought, Davy had been the target of the bully's attempts to hurt someone. He'd been picking at Davy for the past week, something that she wasn't aware of, and he'd punched the other little boy in the face. After knocking him down, apparently, he kicked him in the belly and ribs until he was no longer conscious. No wonder he was so upset; it sounded to her like little Toby would be hurting for a while. He'd been sent to the hospital by ambulance, and that had upset her son, too. An ambulance had meant certain death as far as he was concerned, and that was what had upset him so much.

"We'll call his mom in the morning to see how he's doing." He asked why they couldn't call her now. "It might be too soon. I promise you I'll call first thing in the morning and we'll see how he's doing. Is that all right with you?"

"Yes, I guess so. There was so much blood, Mom. I couldn't believe how bad he was being hurt. It was like he was trying to kill him." She asked about the bully and was ashamed to find out that he'd been knocking her son around for the past two weeks, and she'd not known anything about it. "Toby will be my best friend forever because he took the beating for me. I was going to be hurt, Markus said so, when Toby kicked him in the shin, he took it out on him. He said that I was a bastard boy. I don't know what that means."

"It means that your father was never in the

picture." She was going to call the school in the morning, too, and let them know a piece of her mind. They had to know this was going on, as Davy said that he'd told his teacher every day that he'd be knocked around. Even Toby had tried to tell the teacher. "Your father died. He would have loved to have been here for us, but something happened, and he was taken from us too young."

She held onto Davy for the rest of the night. Every time she got up to go to the bathroom, he would whimper. Maybe she was making him a momma's boy because she was cuddling him so much, but she didn't care tonight. He'd had his heart broken, and she knew only one way to make it better, and that was to be there for him.

After sending him to bed, she knew that he was going to have bad dreams. He'd been mostly upset that his friend had been hurt, but the amount of blood that was surrounding the little boy had scared him. As soon as she knew that the school was open, she gave them a call.

"Mrs. Manchester, boys will be boys. They just had a little scuffle on the playground, and one of them took it too far." She asked how Toby was. "We've not heard anything. The last time we spoke to Mrs. Warfield was when we called her to tell her to meet the ambulance at the hospital."

"You never thought to see if the little boy was all right?" She said that they assumed he was because the medics had said he'd be in the hospital for a couple of days. "My god, he's seven years old. You should have called to tell her that you're taking care of the bully at least. You are, aren't you? Making sure that he's been punished for what he'd done, correct?"

"Like I said to you before, boys will be boys, and things like this happen on the school yard all the time. He'll be fine and back to school before too much longer." She wanted to scream at the woman that wasn't the point, but she hung up on her instead. Calling Toby's mother, she was glad when she answered. Her voice was so solemn that she almost didn't ask how her son was.

"He has a broken wrist and leg. Plus, he has seven broken ribs." She sat down, she felt so guilty by feeling glad that it hadn't been her own son that had been hurt. "His face got the worst of it. He has to have several surgeries to repair the damage done to his cheeks. You should see him. My little boy is a mess, and they have him on all kinds of tubes running into his body to keep him out of pain."

"I'm so sorry. I had no idea it was so bad. Davy told me that there had been a great deal of blood, but I didn't know what had happened." She told her that she was suing the school as soon as she found an attorney who would take her on. "I'm so very sorry about this. If I can do anything, let me know."

"I will. They said that Davy was the one who was in trouble with the boy. I'm so happy for their friendship, but upset that this had to happen. Toby will be in the hospital for weeks now, they told me. I don't have any kind of insurance for anything like this. I just don't know what to do but to sue the school." She didn't agree or disagree with the mom. "Do you know of a good attorney? I sure could use all the help I can get with this."

"I don't know any attorneys at all. I've never had the use for one before." When Mrs. Warfield started to cry, it broke her heart that she couldn't do anything for her. "I'll ask around to see what I can figure out for you. I'm not making any promises, but I will keep my ear out to find one for you. I'm so sorry this happened to you. And with you just moving here and all."

"We came here because we were told that they had a good school system. So far, I'm not seeing it. My husband is fit to be tied." She would bet that he was. She was, and it wasn't even her child. "I have to get off here now. Thank you for calling. If it's all right, I might call you sometime. It's done me a world of good just to be able to vent right now. I just don't know what we're going to do. This wasn't his fault, and now we're going to be up to our eyes in debt because some kid decided to knock the shit out of my son like he was nothing but a rag doll."

After getting off the phone, she decided that she was going to keep Davy home for the day. She didn't want him going to school upset and hearing what had happened to young Toby. She was going to tell him that he'd been hurt really badly, but that's about all. She didn't want him to be upset anymore than he needed to be. As soon as she woke him up to go to daycare, he said that he wanted to go to school. No amount of persuading would keep him from going. He wanted to talk to his other friends about it and be together. She supposed she could understand that. She didn't want to take him, but he needed to go he told her.

Going to work after dropping him off at school, she was nervous all day. When the party of four came in that had stayed so late the other time for lunch, they asked for her. It was all she could do not to beg them to stay late as they had before, because she had an upset child at school and she might have to go get him. But she didn't. When it turned into a party of six, she was glad that she'd stay busy for the afternoon when the school didn't call her.

They were big men and ordered a great deal of food. She was always ready with a smile when she had a big table and got them their food in record time. As soon as all their drinks were refilled, she called the school to see how her son was doing.

"I would have thought that you'd have kept him home today, Mrs. Manchester." She felt like they were shaming her and decided to ignore them for now. "He's with his other little friends, and they've been hanging out together. He still seems to be upset, but not like he had been yesterday." She asked about the bully. "Tommy? He's fine. He's in class right now. Why would you ask?"

"Because he beat a little boy nearly to death yesterday. Aren't you going to do anything about him?" She said that again. That boys will be boys, and there was no harm done. "He's going to be in the hospital for weeks now. He has broken ribs and a wrist, and a leg. His mother told me that he's going to need more surgeries on his little face because of what Tommy did. You think that's normal for boys to be?"

"I don't know what it is you're upset about. Nothing happened to your boy. Just stay out of it before we have to make sure that Davy doesn't go to school here anymore." She said that she couldn't do that. "We have ways of getting rid of the bad apples. You just keep your opinion to yourself and not call here again, making accusations that you can't cover." Then the line went dead.

Going outside so that she could breathe, Lisa thought about what was just said to her. Her son was considered a bad apple, and this Tommy boy was getting away with almost murder. She wanted to hurt someone now, but knew that she'd only be causing Davy more trouble. Plastering a smile on her face, she went back in to finish her job for the day. Good thing she didn't have to work tonight, or she might just get fired for taking her frustrations out on a patron. Just as she entered the dining room again, one of the men from the table came to find her.

"I'm sorry. I didn't mean to neglect you. What is it you need?" He just stared at her. "Sir? Is there something wrong? I assure you that I can fix it if you have found something wrong with things."

"What's your name?" She told him her name was Lisa, and that was all. "Hello, Lisa. I'm sorry for this, but I belong to you."

"I don't understand." He then explained how he'd heard her on the phone and was worried about her. "It's something to do with an incident yesterday. One of the little boys at my son's school was badly injured."

"You have a son, too? That's wonderful." She was sort of being creeped out by the man and asked him again what she could do for him. "Nothing yet. I mean, this is all still new to me, and I don't want to frighten you. What do you know about shifters?"

"Nothing much. Is there anything I can do for

you at the table?" He shook his head and smiled at her. "I'm having a really bad day, sir. If you could just tell me what's going on, I can help you with it. Otherwise, I'm going to have to ask you to back off."

"I can do that." He took several steps back, only to take two forward. "I'm your mate. Do you know what that is?"

"Something about you owning me." He said it was nothing like that at all, but that she owned him. Heart and soul. "You're beginning to make me feel uncomfortable. I'm going to have to ask you to go back to your seat."

"All right. But we should talk. I want to tell you that if you're having trouble with the school, I can help you out with that. I used to be an attorney at one time. I don't want anything to happen to you or your boy." She just nodded to him and wondered what was wrong with him. "I'll stay after you get off so that we can talk. I know you must have questions."

"What I have is a creepy feeling that you're stalking me. I want you to go and sit down." He said that he would and went to the table. She knew she was blowing her tip by not being extra nice to the man, but she was genuinely freaked out by him and didn't know what to do. "Go have a seat, please."

He went back to his seat, and she noticed that all the men were now staring at her with an odd smile.

She could handle them if she wanted to and decided that she was going to give them the best service that she could. Even if all six were making her feel a little uncomfortable by the way they were staring at her.

Chapter 2

Brenin couldn't believe his luck. He'd not even wanted to go to the diner when he'd been invited, and now he'd found his mate. She was a little skittish, but he thought that was just his fault. He'd been a little forward in talking to her, and now she was afraid of him. He didn't like that feeling that he'd given her, but it couldn't be helped right now. He was going to make it up to her by talking to her. He also wanted to know what was going on with the school and how he could help her with that. He'd heard both ends of the conversation as the woman on the other end of the line had been loud. Something about a little boy beaten nearly to death, and he was now in the hospital.

"What are you going to do?" Of course, they would ask him that. His brother, especially. "She's a little freaked out by you." Tucker would know about that as he'd freaked out his own mate when he'd found her.

"I know. That's my fault. I shouldn't have come on so strong to her." Tank asked about the phone call. "I don't know, but I'm going to find out. It has really upset her. Something about another little boy. She has a son, too, I heard."

They had finished eating and were getting ready to leave. He was glad that he'd driven himself to the little restaurant, so now he could wait for her to be finished so that he could talk to her. Excitement made him a little giddy, but he was trying his best to refrain from upsetting her anymore. After paying the bill, they all put money on the table in the form of a tip. She was going to do well today, as they all knew she was his mate.

He knew that he couldn't wait at the table for her, so he went out to his car and waited for her to get off. He had no idea how long that was going to be, but he'd wait all night if necessary. At about a quarter after four, she was coming out of the place and headed towards her car. He stood back until she had her door open before he spoke to her.

"I'm so sorry that I upset you in the restaurant." She held her keys in front of her with one key between her knuckles. "You're right to be cautious. It's good to know that you're not taking any chances. But I'd rather die than to hurt you."

"What do you want? I have to pick up my son, and I'm already late." He asked if she had a few minutes they could talk. "I don't know what there is to say. I don't want to be your mate, and that's final. I've had a husband before, and while he was a good man when we were married, he left me a widow, and I can't forgive him for that."

"I won't leave you behind." She said that everyone dies. "Not me. Not you either, now that I've found you. Nor will your son. He'll be all right so long as he lives to be about twenty, then he won't age anymore. Neither will—I'm doing this all wrong. I'm sorry. I'd like to talk to you when you can allow me to do that."

"What do you mean he won't die, and neither will I? Everyone dies at some point in their lives." He said that they were all immortals. "I don't want to be an immortal if that means I have to allow you to rule over me."

"I don't know why everyone thinks that we're going to rule our mates. I have no intentions of doing anything like that. If you'd like to continue working like you are, then I will be supportive and there for you. But you don't have to work another day in your life, and we'd be fine with money." Again, he thought he was doing this wrong and took in a deep breath, letting it out slowly. "My name is Brenin Savage. I'm sure you've heard of the Savage men."

"They have all the money in the world." He said that was him; he was one of them. "Why should I believe you? For all I know, you think to rob me of my tips today."

"I don't need your money either. I have plenty. Not as much as is in the world, but I'm wealthy beyond anything we can spend in our lives together." She didn't lower the weapon of her keys, and he didn't blame her. He was beginning to sound like a lunatic even to himself. "You said you have to go and get your son. Let's do that, and we'll talk. I can either ride with you or meet you at your house. Either one is fine with me."

"I have to get Davy." He said that he understood her and that he'd meet her at her house. "All right. I have no idea why I trust you not to hurt me, but I do. If you so much as talk to Davy badly, I will rip your throat out and kill you."

"I would allow it." After getting her address, he said he'd met her at her home. He waited until she was in her car and gone before he got into his own car and left. She was afraid of him, and that broke his heart. He'd never hurt her or her son, and he needed to have her know that soon. As soon as he pulled up in front of the house, he realized what a nice neighborhood she lived in. All the little houses were in neat rows with good lawns and nicely trimmed trees. He could see himself living here if it came to that. He'd live anywhere she wished so long as she trusted him.

It took her an hour to get home. He had a feeling that she'd been having second thoughts and wasn't going to come home. But he stuck it out and stayed and was glad that he had to see little Davy. He looked just like his mom and thought that anyone could see it. As he made his way up to the house, when she got out and opened the door, he was careful where he tread so that she'd not be afraid of him again.

"This is my son, Davy Manchester. Davy, this is Mr. Savage. He's going to be leaving soon. He wants to talk to me." Davy asked if he had to do his homework, and she told him that he did. It was just going over his site words again, she told him, and she was proud of him when he got them all right. Lisa told him that her son would be in second grade next year, as he'd only just turned seven, and she knew that he was doing well in school. "Put your things away, please, before you do your homework."

"Nice to meet you, young man." Davy shook his hand and told him it was a pleasure to meet him. As soon as the introductions were made, he hung up his coat and got out his words. "I can help you with them while your mom makes you dinner if you want. Or I can talk to her while she does that."

"We're having spaghetti tonight. It's my second favorite meal." He asked what his first was, and he told him about the burger place on Maple. "I eat there when we have extra money for a treat."

"Davy, he doesn't care what we do for treats."

He didn't say anything but was going to be happy for any kind of information he could get about either of them. "Do your words, and Mr. Savage and I will talk in the kitchen. How was school today?"

"Better than yesterday." That was all he said, and he thought that whatever had happened at the school had traumatized the boy quite a bit. He shivered when his mom asked how his day had gone. "Toby wasn't at school or after school today. I missed him."

"We'll talk about him later." Davy seemed satisfied with that, and Brenin went to the kitchen with Lisa. She had sauce on the stove already simmering. He thought for sure it was homemade and would have loved to have been invited to eat if he hadn't eaten so much at the diner. "What is it you wish to talk to me about? I won't have you ruling me while I'm in my own home either."

"I wouldn't dream of it. You seem to have a really nice place here." She said that it was home. "I just bought a house that I'm working on. It needed the kitchen updated, but that's about finished right now. It had to be taken to the studs so that the wiring could be redone." He was babbling and didn't understand why. "I'm going to tell you a little bit about myself. Then you can tell me whatever it is that you wish to tell me about yourself."

"I won't be your slave either." He told her that

he didn't need slaves and had been around when they were very popular and wouldn't do that to anyone. "You make it sound like you're older than you look. I'm assuming that you're hundreds of years old."

"Thousands of years old. I'm the youngest of the two of us. I have a brother named Cassian who just found his mate. They're happy together." She didn't say anything, and he continued telling her about himself. "I've been around for a long time, as I said, and I've been happier than I've been in the last few months. My parents are both dead, as is my sister. Other than Cassian, I have a lot to do with my cousins. We all grew up together."

"What are you? You told me that you were a shifter, so what is it that you can shift into?" He told her that he was a blue dragon. "I didn't know there were any dragons that were real, much less colored ones."

"My younger cousin, Tucker, is a red dragon. He burns hot all the time, while my brother and I are both running cold all the time." She nodded once, and he continued. "As I said, we've been around for a long time and have amassed a fortune in money and investments. So when I said that you'd not have to work unless you wanted to, I was telling you the truth. By the way, I can't lie to you. About anything. Nor will I ever hurt you intentionally."

"I don't believe you. I'm sorry if that's harsh, but I have a hard time believing that you're going to expect anything of me other than to rule me and make me your slave. I'm stronger than I look, so if you try anything, I'm going to kill you. It might be hard, but I will hurt you at least." He said he'd have it no other way. "Why are you being so nice to me? I've just told you that I'm going to kill you if you try anything, and you said it was all right."

"Because I'd rather die than to harm you, rule you, or to make you my slave. I have no intentions of doing any of those things so long as you give me a chance to try to prove to you that I'm just what I said I am. A man who happens to be able to shift into a dragon that will love you forever." She asked him if he was saying that he loved her. "I am. I might not know you well enough right now to proclaim that I do indeed love you, but I'm falling in love with you more with each minute that we spend together."

"That's just not right. You have to know that." He nodded and watched her as she put the noodles in the pot of boiling water. "I don't know what to say about any of this."

"That's all right. I can understand. This is a lot to take in right now." She asked him if he was staying for dinner. "If you'd not mind. I don't know how much I can eat, but it smells delicious."

He ended up eating two plates of pasta. He'd been right in thinking that she'd made the sauce herself. By the time dinner was over, he helped her clean up. It was the least he could do after she'd invited him to dinner. After Davy had his bath and was ready for bed, she sat him down and told him about the little boy named Toby.

"He might not be back to school for a while yet. He's been hurt really bad." He asked if he was going to die. "I don't think so. He's in good hands at the hospital, but he's going to need to be there for a while yet. When he's better, we'll go and see him. All right?"

"He took the beating for me. I will love him forever." She told him that was good and to make sure when he said his prayers tonight, he asked God to keep him safe and to get well. "I will, Mom. I love you."

"And I love you too, my darling little man." He thought that she said that to her son a great deal, as he didn't get embarrassed when she said it to him. After he was put in his bed, telling him good night, too, the two of them went to the living room to talk more. He was willing to do whatever it took to get her to trust him, and that meant showing her his dragon soon so that she'd know he would never harm her. "I have to get up early in the morning, so let's make this quick. I don't want to like you, but for some reason, I trust you not to lie to me. I don't know about any of the other stuff that I've said to you."

"I understand." The two of them talked for about another hour before he left. He was excited to see her again, but wasn't going to rush her into anything. As soon as he left, he felt better than he had in a long time. He had a mate, and she was going to be the best thing that had ever happened to him. At least he hoped so.

~*~

Lisa didn't know what to do with herself. She'd been entertaining a man last night, and now today all she could think about was how stupid she felt. First of all? Where did the word *entertaining* come from? Was she sixty-something years old? They'd had dinner together, and he left. He had helped clean up, which she didn't think meant entertaining at all. Something was wrong with her today, and she couldn't quite put her finger on what it was.

Getting ready for work after dropping her son off at school, she decided that since she had to work later in the day, if it came up for her to work the dinner schedule, she would. Just so she'd have the extra hours. But she'd have to miss Davy, and that always made her day better when she could see him before he went to bed.

Work was busy, and she had enough in tips for the week to make it so she didn't have to work tonight. It was just as well; she would have had to have Davy at a sitter, and that would eat into whatever profits she made by working extra. Her boss said that she didn't need anyone extra tonight, and she looked so sad. It worried her that the place would be closing down soon, as it just wasn't doing that much in the way of business anymore.

She'd been working at the restaurant since she'd had Davy. When she'd first started working, she made good money, enough that she didn't have to work a second job. But now if she didn't grade papers for the school, she wouldn't be able to afford her rent, much less food for the table and all the extras like school fees and babysitting. Some weeks, she about broke even when it came to income and outgoing money.

The insurance policy that her husband had on himself if he were killed didn't pay all that much. She'd had to share it with his mom as she'd been named on the policy too. That had taken away most of the money that would have gone to buying them a stable home and a good car. As it was now, she was still driving the car that they'd had when they first got married, and the house was a rental. Janice had insisted that she give her half of the only income that she'd had from her husband dying so young, and she wasn't sure why Janice needed it. She didn't seem to have a job, nor did she have any other work-related issues when it came to income. She told Lisa it was because he'd named her on it that she deserved it. She supposed that was right, but it didn't help her with her life and that of Davy.

One of the first things that she paid for monthly was the insurance she had on herself and her son. And as soon as he was married, she was going to insist that they take her name off the policy so that in the event something happened to him, she'd have whatever she needed to get by. It's what Janice should have done when they were first married. It would have made her life a whole lot better.

Then she was forever bringing up how she was supporting the two of them. The only thing that she'd ever done for them was to cause trouble. Davy didn't like the way she treated him when she was around, and she couldn't get it out of her head that Davy was a growing boy and didn't necessarily like spending the night with her anymore. She wasn't going to make him spend the night either. That would be just wrong. She was just too needy all the time.

When work was over, she made her way to the grocery store. Davy wanted to have hot dogs for dinner, and she needed to get some buns. Not that he ever ate the bun, but she liked them and was going to pick some up. As soon as she paid and was headed out the door, a woman came in and stopped her. She said her name was Kaida Savage.

"It's nice to meet you. Do you come here often?"

She said that she usually went to the store up the road, as it had more variety, but when she just needed something, she stopped here. "I'm cousin-in-law to Brenin. He said that he met you."

"We're working things out. I have my life just the way that I want it, and I'm afraid that he'll want more of my time than I'm willing to give to him." She simply nodded but didn't try to convince her otherwise. "I have to get going. I'm going to pick up Davy, and we're headed home."

"Yes, of course. I just wanted to meet you, and I'm glad that I have. I don't usually shop here, but today, like you, I needed something extra for dinner. It was nice meeting you." She shook hands with the woman and felt an electrical shock go up her arm. Thinking nothing of it, she went out to her car and started it. Her arms were still buzzing when she put the car into drive and stopped moving.

Something was off. She knew that the daycare was just down the road from her, but she couldn't make herself go. Just as she was thinking about how ridiculous she was making things out to be, a large SUV pulled into the lot at about fifty miles per hour and would have hit her had she been sitting at the light. As it was, he rolled his car, and it landed on its top. Scared out of her mind, she turned the car off and sat there thinking how she would have been hit had she moved forward when she got into the car.

"Are you all right?" Lisa turned and looked at the woman standing at her door. She couldn't for the life of her remember who she was. "It's Kaida Savage. We just met a few minutes ago. Are you all right? Please say something."

"I would have been there had I not paused." She looked at the accident where people were gathered now and back at the woman. "I didn't feel right going ahead, so I waited. I would have been there had I gone forward."

"Let me get into the car with you." She nodded and unlocked the door so that she could get in with her. "Just turn off the engine, and we'll sit here and talk. I gave you something. Unless you had this kind of magic before?"

"I don't have any magic now." Nodding once, she reached over and turned off the car. "I would have been there. I can't get that out of my head. But it just didn't feel right, and I was getting ready to go again, and it happened. I'm sorry. I don't know what to think."

"It saved your life, whatever magic you got from me." She said she didn't have any magic. "Then what do you call this near miss that you just had. I saw you. You did hesitate when you got into the car. I saw you about ready to go forward, too. You're right in thinking that you would have been hurt."

"What do you mean you gave me something? When we were talking last night, Brenin said that same thing. That he more than likely gave me some of his magic. I don't believe in magic any more than I do… the next thing you're going to tell me is that there are vampires and unicorns around." She said that there were both, and she'd show them to her sometime. "I don't know what to believe. This is all so…I could be dead if I had gone forward."

"You'd not be dead, but you'd be in a world of hurt. You're immortal as of the moment that Brenin found you. Or you found him. I'm not sure how it worked out for the two of you." Nodding, not sure now if she really would have been hit or not. "Don't do that. Don't make it out to be nothing when we both know that it was. I'm going to contact Brenin and let him know that you're safe. He'll understand the rest of it."

"I have to pick up my son." She said she'd have to wait a moment until things calmed down in her heart. "I'm just fine now. I've had time to think about what might have happened, and I feel better. I wouldn't have been hurt at all."

But in her mind, she knew that to be a lie. All she would have been able to do is look at the SUV rolled on its top to know that she would have been killed. He'd not just gone through the light that she'd been sitting at, but he took out the stop light as well as hit the little car that she would have been behind when it came at her. Laying her head on the steering wheel, she inhaled slowly and exhaled the same way. Slow breathing was helping her cope.

"Come on and let's get out of the car. You might feel better if you were to stand up for a few minutes." Nodding, she not only got out of the car but also made sure that her purse was over her arm. She needed things to be normal for a few minutes, or she was going to go insane thinking about what could have been. "Just breathe. You'll see, you're doing fine now. Just breathe in and out for a bit."

"I'm better now. So long as I don't think about what could have happened, I'm better." She nodded but didn't look convinced. "Really. I'm just going to keep telling myself that I was lucky that I had to put my purse on the seat next to me. That's what caused me to pause. There wasn't any kind of feeling like I was going to be hurt or something along those lines. I'm fine, and that's all I know. Did you get in touch with Brenin?"

"He's on his way. He's with my husband, Tucker. You've not met any of the others yet, have you?" Telling her that she'd barely met Brenin had her thinking again, and she didn't want to think. Instead, she looked at her watch and realized that she was still early to pick up Davy. What if he'd been in the car with her when that happened?

"Oh my. I think I'm going to be sick." She leaned over and threw up what she'd had for lunch at work. Entitled to one meal when she worked a shift, she was glad to have it. It not only saved her money in the long run but— "I don't think I'm right in the head. I keep thinking of these random things and then the accident again. It's like my mind is on a loop of some sort."

"You're doing fine. Much better than I think I would had I just avoided a major accident. Look, there's the men now." She looked up and saw Brenin coming toward her, and all she could think about was that he was going to make things right for her. "She's had a terrible fright."

As soon as he pulled her into his arms, she knew that she was all right, and her mind seemed to settle down. Like he just held her steady. While she didn't know where that feeling was coming from, she wasn't going to question it right now. She didn't get hurt, and that was the big outcome of all of this. And Davy was safe too.

"Something is going on. I don't know what it is, but there is something wrong with me." He asked her what she thought it was. "I don't know. All I know is since I've met you, my world has turned upside-down and not in a good way."

"It's the magic that you got. If you're not used to it, it'll take some getting used to. You should be able to change your clothing with just a thought, too. I should have mentioned that last night when I was talking to you. It happened to me today." She asked him what else might happen. "I don't know what else you might have gotten from all of us. It's different with each woman who comes to the family. However, I do know that you can shift into a dragon. That was a gift from the lady earth when she said she owed us a gift for helping her out with the faeries."

"Enough. Please." He nodded, then smiled at her. "You're not as charming as you might think you are. I don't want to know anything else right now. I have to pick up my son, and then I think we'll go get burgers. He'll like that better than hot dogs anyway. Then I'm going home. I have stuff to do."

"Can I come with you?" She nodded before she thought about him being in the mix of her day. "I'll not bring up anything unless you ask. I promise."

"Good. Not even if you see something. Unless I ask, I'm going to assume that it didn't happen and that I'm all right. Just a regular person who has had a strange day." She looked once more at where the police were with the SUV. There were ambulances there now, and she couldn't help but think once again that she'd been killed had she been there. "Nothing out of the ordinary happened, and I'm all right. I'm going to get my son. Are you coming?"

"Yes. I'll drive if you don't mind. You seem still a little off." She told him she was fine and that she was all right with him driving. "We'll just go up the street to turn into the daycare. All right?"

"Yes. It's the one right there on Maple Avenue." Going in to get her son, she was glad for his hugs on so many levels that she didn't know what to do about it. Her mind was still racing, but she had a handle on it now. As soon as she told Davy they were having burgers tonight, he was excited. It wasn't often she could make him happy about a change in plans, but she'd been able to do that today. Going inside with Brenin at her side felt normal, but she wasn't going to say that to him. It had already been a strange day, and she wasn't going to add to it if she didn't have to.

Chapter 3

Brenin watched Lisa carefully. She seemed to be just fine one moment, then she'd drift off and shiver the next. Like she was reliving the accident that didn't happen because of magic. When Davy was ready for bed, she read him a story and tucked him in. When she came back to the living room, he could tell that she'd come to a decision, and he was almost afraid of what it would be.

"Tell me again about me being your mate and what kind of magic I'm supposed to get." He opened his mouth, but she held up her hand. "I don't want to know about sex or how it makes us stronger right now. I'm taking this one step at a time, and I don't want to get too ahead of myself and get all bogged down with details I don't need just yet. Just give me the basics."

The first thing he told her about was changing her clothing at will. "You should just be able to think of something that you want to wear, and you'll have it on. Even if it's just sweatpants or a designer dress, you'll have it on. It doesn't cost you anything either, in the event you were going to ask."

"I wasn't, but that's good to know. So I can just

want woolly socks on my feet, and they'll be there?" He asked her if she wanted to try yet. "Not yet. I'm still trying to wrap my mind around stuff, and trying it out would bog me down again. What about this premonition thing? Was that a one-shot deal or should I expect it to be around forever?"

"I don't know. Sometimes, women get more than we give them simply by being around the rest of the dragons. I did tell you I was a dragon, didn't I?" She said he might have mentioned it, but she didn't remember. "I'm a blue dragon. I'm cold most of the time. Tucker, my younger cousin, is a red dragon. He burns hot all the time. But when I told you that you could shift that has nothing to do with me. Except that you'll be able to shift into a dragon. The Lady Earth did that for us as a gift."

"I remember now. You said it was to help with the faeries." He told her that it was right. Keeping an eye on her, he was happy that she seemed less stressed out. But he didn't know her that well yet, and she might be stressed out, and he didn't know it. "Will Davy have magic, too? I'm not sure that I'd be happy with him having magic. He's only seven years old."

"He'll more than likely be able to change his clothing at will. I agree with you on the magic, but I have no way of knowing what he'll get. Or what he has now. The Lady Earth could tell us, but she'd have to come here, and I'm not sure you're ready for that just yet. She has wings and a halo around her. She's very beautiful. Not as beautiful as you are right now, but she's lovely." She asked what sort of magic her son might get again. "We'll cross that bridge when we get to it. All right?"

"Yes, all right. If I don't tell him about it, he'll not try it at school and get himself into trouble. That's the way I'm going to handle it right now." He thought that was an excellent idea and told her that. "I do have them on occasion. It's just today, I'm a little lost on where the ideas are coming from. I'm sick with worry if you want to know the truth. What if you decided that I'm not for you, or Davy isn't in the picture? He's my life, and I will not send him away because you have some kind of dislike about him not being your son."

"I would love him like he's my own child. And if you and I were to have any more children, I would treat him no differently than I treat the other kids." She didn't want to believe him, but he said he couldn't lie to her. Like she believed that he'd never lie to her. Everyone lied, and it was just a fact of life. "I can see you're thinking hard on something, and I wish you'd ask me rather than ponder it out on your own."

"I'm fine. What about sex? Are you going to force it on me even though you said you'd not rule me?" He seemed hesitant at first, but then he told her it was her body and she was the only one who would decide if they had sex or not. "Don't count on it happening too soon then. I'm not sure I even like you right now. You seem to be just too calm."

"I'm usually the calm one in the bunch. I've always been." She asked him what he was calm about. "Anything and everything. I don't let things get to me either. If I can't resolve something in a reasonable time, I ask for help, or I walk away for a little while so that I can get my head on straight. I don't know how I'll do with you and Davy, but I will remain calm as long as I can about something. I will protect the two of you with my life and my dragon."

"Will I get to see him sometime? Not now. I don't know how big he is, and we have nosy neighbors." He told her that there wasn't even enough room in her backyard for him to shift and not allow the neighbors to see. "I don't want them knowing that I'm dating or whatever this is called between the two of us. They'll tell Janice, and she'll react badly. Even though it's been almost eight years, she'll still think I should be holding out for her son for some reason. Not that I want you to spend the night just yet, but we'll work on that when the timing is better."

"I have a house. It's a nice one that is being worked on right now. It needed a new roof, and they should be finished with that in a few days. Also, the kitchen has been updated. I don't cook much, but I'm home a great deal, so I have a staff as well. If you wish to continue to work, then they'll be helpful around the house. Or if you'd rather live here, that's fine too." She told him she'd have to see it and the school district he's in. "I understand. If it helps any, we're in the same district as you are here. He'd get to ride the bus, however, because he's outside the city limits at our house in town."

"He'd love that. A few of his friends live outside the city limits and get to ride the bus. He'll think that's the best reason ever to move. I'm not saying I'm ready to move in with you, and if I do, then I'll pay my share of the house payment too."

"You have no reason to work, I think I told you that before. I have enough money that neither one of us has to work another day in our long lives. I have to work because I think I would go crazy if I didn't. I need to keep my mind busy, too." She said that she was barely making it as it is right now with two jobs. "I would have thought you'd be getting some kind of widow's pension from when your husband was killed."

"He was off duty when he was killed." He said he didn't think it mattered, but he'd look into it if she didn't mind. "I wouldn't mind. Janice took half of his insurance policy. It wasn't all that much, just ten grand, but it would have gone a long way in paying for his funeral. As it stands right now, I'm making monthly payments to that. I should have stepped in more when his mom was making arrangements, and I might not have such a big bill, but she wanted it all, including extra calling hours, and I was too shocked to know anything about it until later."

"I'm sorry she took half of his money. Did she have a reason for that?" She told him how her name was on the policy and that she didn't have to give her any of it. "No, I guess not, but that seems sort of selfish to me. I would have wanted to make sure you had it all."

"I never understood her reasons either. She told me that I was just lucky that she was in a generous mood, or I wouldn't have gotten that much. I never saw the policy myself, but she took care that we had half of it." Brenin didn't think that was right and made a mental note to look into it. He would never have done anything like that. In fact, he'd given away an insurance policy worth millions to Ace and Tank when they were found after his parents and sister had been killed by the council. "If you find out anything, don't say anything to Davy. He's not into caring for his grandmother too much as it is. She's been wanting things from him that he's not willing to let her have. Like spending the night and cuddling with her on the couch. He does it here, but then I don't make a big deal about it like she does."

They talked until midnight, and he was glad for it. He had a few things he was going to be doing for her and others that he was going to make sure got looked into. He couldn't believe that the older Mrs. Manchester would do that to her son's wife, but stranger things had happened. When he said that he'd walk to his car, he really didn't want her to wake up Davy to take him back to it; he told her he'd be fine. He was a dragon after all.

He didn't have any trouble and called her when he got to the car as soon as he got into it. She made him promise that he'd call her when he got home, too, and he did it. The house seemed so empty now that he was alone in it, and he wondered how it would be filled with laughter when Davy and Lisa lived there. He was looking forward to that more than anything.

The next morning, he was making notes on the conversations that he'd had with her and was glad that he could look things up on the computer. Having the application that would do background checks was the first thing he did. Janice Manchester was right there for him to see all that she was about.

The first thing that he noticed was that she'd cashed a fifty-thousand-dollar policy on her husband when he had died nineteen years ago. That was quite a bit of money back then, and she'd invested well. The second bit of income that she had that wasn't her monthly checks was another insurance policy from her son, David Manchester. It was much more than the one from her husband and was worth just over two million dollars. Saying that she gave her daughter-in-law half was a lie.

On top of that, she owned the house that Lisa was renting, and it looked like she'd just raised her rent. There was something fishy going on with the elderly woman, and he was going to see what he could find out by sending a faerie to her home and see what was going on. He told himself it was just to watch over the woman, but it was more than that. He no longer trusted her at her word, and she'd never even spoken to him. The rent thing bothered him the most. Why would she be charging her rent at all?

The more he looked into her life, the stranger things got. Like she had a wealth of money that was just sitting in the bank. Why wasn't she helping out with her grandson more? She had to know that Lisa was struggling with two jobs that barely made a dent in her rent now that it had been raised again. Then there were the insurance policies that she was paying for, not to mention the insurance on them in the event that they needed a doctor.

Each time he found something, he'd be amazed

that she wasn't helping out with Lisa more. Or, at the very least, not charge her rent each month on the house she was renting. It was like she was making it so that she failed. When that thought popped into his head, he knew that was exactly what it was. She was making her have to come to her for help and was holding out on her for some reason.

That thought was centered in his mind when he found that there were two more policies taken out on Lisa and Davy for millions of dollars. Using his considerable magic, he called for help with Lady Earth to see what she might know about the elderly woman.

"I know nothing more than you have there before you. I will look deeper into her lands. She doesn't plant any flowers around her home, much like the others have surrounding her. But I never thought that she could be doing it for selfish reasons. The other people around her have begged her to help out by keeping her yard maintained, but she just won't do it. It has been a sore spot in their lives when they try to sell their homes. With hers looking so poorly, their houses aren't worth as much as they could get from them." He asked her how she would know that. "I have my reasons for watching over the place. Much violence had gone on there before the husband finally passed away. He was an abused spouse. We have been keeping an eye on the house for many decades, and the faeries know better than to be caught there, too. Yes, much violence has been at that address. You said that your mate is related to her by marriage? She would do well not to trust the woman. She's also been known to hurt herself on purpose so that your mate must see to her needs. It hasn't happened as much as it did in the past, but it does happen sometimes."

"You've given me a great deal of information that I wouldn't have gotten from the web. Thank you so much." She said she was very welcome to be able to help him. "I'll have to keep an eye on her myself. I think she's making it so that my mate will have to go to her soon for help with her money. She won't want to, but she'll have no choice."

"Then you should bring her to your home before it gets to that. Show her what a beautiful dragon she has in you, and make sure that she can see her own. It will be such a great gift to me to see the two of you flying in the sky again." He asked if she'd seen them all lately. "Yes, I come to the flying when I can. With so much time on my hands now, I feel like I can do lots of things that I never did before. Seeing my dragons fly is one of the best treasures that I have. I so love to see you all flying."

He'd have to look for her the next time they were all flying. And invite her to join them. He was sure she could fly, too, and that would be a rare treat for them as well. Making notes on the things that he wanted to tell Lisa, he was armed with enough information that would keep her safe from the old woman.

~*~

When Brenin came by with the file an hour ago, she didn't have time to look it over. He did tell her that her rent was going to go up, and not ten minutes after he left, she got the certified mail that told her that it was going to be raised to two hundred dollars a month. That was more than she'd been expecting it to raise. Sitting down with the file now that she had time, she was having a hard time adjusting to the idea that Janice was the one who owned her home and was the person she made her checks out to each month. Then to raise it so much was unheard of. Why was she doing this to her?

Brenin returned with dinner and some photos of his home. He asked her to go see it with him, but not tonight. She had to grade papers and still get ready for working a double shift tomorrow. He seemed to understand, but that didn't negate the fact that Janice was trying to ruin her. She asked him what he thought was going on.

"She's trying to make you beholden to her is all I can think about. You told me once that she tried to get you two to move in with her. She's just making it so you have to now. And with the rent going up, it looks to me like she's getting desperate for you to do just that." She said that she could take another job, but that would cut into her time with her son. "I believe she wants that too. To make sure that she's there to babysit your son. Again, for you to be beholden to her. She doesn't need the money. She has a great deal of that on her own. Not as much as we all do, but she didn't need you to continue paying rent to her after her son died."

"She's lied to me about so much, I don't know what to believe from her anymore. I mean, she said that the policy was only for ten grand, and I can see a copy of it right here that says differently. Why would she do that to us? It's not like we've done anything to her." He said he didn't know what was in her mind, but was glad he'd been able to find it all. "I am as well. I just don't know what I'm supposed to do with this information."

"I know one solution to your problem. And I'm not rushing you into anything other than to feel better about helping you. You could either move into my house with me, no strings attached, or I can pay your rent for you. It wouldn't be that big of a hardship on me to make that work for you." In all honesty, she didn't know how she was going to make that work in the first place. Even getting a third job was going to be difficult with having Davy. He would be at the sitters' more than he would be at home. "Anything you make at a third job will be eaten away in putting Davy in daycare of some kind. I could watch over him, too, if you didn't mind. He's going to be my son someday, and this would be a way that we could get to know one another."

"Don't get ahead of yourself just yet." He smiled and said he was sorry. "Again, no charming me out of things. I have a lot on my mind right now. How could she do this to us? There isn't any reason at all that I can think of other than what you said about us being beholden to her. Did I tell you that she's been trying to get us to move in with her? She's been hinting about it a great deal of late. I just don't know what to do about this from her."

She didn't either. It was as if she were being pulled apart about what she should be doing. Getting a third job wasn't feasible. Not that it would do her much good. Every cent of it would have to go to paying for a sitter for him because there was no way she was going to ask Janice to do it for her. That would be a disaster just waiting to happen. Davy would hate her, and she'd be stuck in the middle again.

"I can't make it work in my head about the rent going up. She's trying to ruin us by jacking it up to this much so that I can't afford it and go to her either for a loan to get by with or to move in with her. Neither one of those is something that I can live with. Not now, especially." She looked at Brenin. "If we move in with you, and that's a big if, if we move in with you, there will be rules that we all have to follow. I will stay with you in a separate bedroom. I don't know where that might lead down the road, but for now, I must insist on that being the number one rule. The second one is that Davy might have to stay with you, but there are going to be rules for that, too. He can't go to you for something that I might not want him to do."

"I would never do that to the two of you. He's your son, and I understand that." She asked about the other. "I have an eight-bedroom house. You can both have as much room as you need. I've never slept in the master suite, so you can have that. I've been bedding down in one of the smaller bedrooms while they were working on the master, and I just got used to it. Davy can have any other room that he wants."

"Moving out is going to be hard for both of us. Davy has lived here his entire life and knows nothing else." He said that he could understand that as well. "You're being too nice to me again. Aren't you the least bit upset about this? I am. I'm so pissed right now that I want to hunt Janice down and beat her to a pulp. I won't because that's not in my nature, but I'm pissed off at her."

"Might I suggest we have the faeries move you. That way, you can be moved in one load, and she'll be none the wiser about it until it's over." She asked how that would work. "They're very magical and would be able to move things around in no time at all. Once you're moved out, you can tell her if you want. But frankly, without you knowing that she's your landlord, it wouldn't be any of her business what you do with your home."

"True. I like the idea of moving out all in one day. It will be hard enough living between two places when the trucks arrive. This will make it so that we don't have to move all that much either. Not with their help." She looked around the room they were in. "There isn't much here that I care to take with me, to be honest. Somehow, it's all tainted because of what she's done to make it happen. I mean, you must be pissed too. Your hand is being forced, and that's something that I can't get over either."

They talked about what would go and what would stay. He got with his own faerie to see how difficult it would be for them to move the things out of Davy's room, and she said it wouldn't be anything at all. They'd just make things small for them to carry so that they could put them in the new house when they arrive. It sounded too easy to be true, but she believed the little woman.

Her next day off was tomorrow, and while Davy was at school, they were going to move. The faeries were set to help, and she was excited to be able to pull the wool over Janice's eyes. To think all this time she'd been feeling sorry for the elderly woman, and all along she'd been hurting them financially. And she'd lied to them both about so many things that she wanted to call her out on them, but decided that she was going to let her stew in her own soup for a while. It would be wonderful to have help with Davy and the house payment, but she was more looking forward to having her time with her son while he was still enjoying her being around.

The next morning dawned bright and early. She didn't tell Davy that they were moving because she was afraid it would get around the school what she was doing. He would be upset for a little while, but once he saw that his room hadn't changed all that much and he was going to get to ride the bus from now on, he'd think of it as an adventure. She hoped so anyway. She hated to sneak around, but it was the only way that things could work out, so she didn't have to work so hard.

The move was much easier than she thought it would be. As soon as the pip, she knew what that meant how showed up, they were ready to get to work. Davy's room was moved with the faeries, and the house was empty in no time. She was going to use some of the furniture in her bedroom to fill out some spaces in the master suite at the new house, and everything in the cabinets was gone before she realized it was time for lunch. They ate it on the way to his home, and she didn't have to eat a burger either.

"I rarely pick out where I'm going to have a meal. I let Davy decide because we do it so seldom." Brenin said that he rarely eats at home anymore because it's so lonely. "I can understand that, too. Sometimes when I'm at home and Davy is at school, I skip meals so that I don't have to eat alone. It's not just boring but sort of sad too."

"Yes, exactly." He laughed, and she joined him. "The house is a big one. As I told you before, we have staff, so you don't have to worry about keeping up with it. It's all done by the faeries that live there. They have their own room at the house too, I forgot to mention." She asked him if it was one with lots of lights. "Windows for sure. They seem to like having lots of sunlight, and I find that I don't care so long as the house is maintained. The first time I realized that they were cleaning up after me, I noticed the windows and the lack of dust. They were sparkling clean, and there were no more dust bunnies around. I've gotten spoiled with having them around for all kinds of reasons. That's just the top two."

On the way to his house, she was nervous. She'd never seen the house, and now she was going to be living in it with him. Not in the same bed, not yet, but in the same house was a big change for her. Davy would have to get used to it as well. There being another male around might do him some good, too. As soon as she inspected the rooms, she was glad for the master suite as it was close to where Davy was sleeping. Only a couple of doors down from where he was.

Picking up Davy from school, he was excited to see her. Apparently, the teacher had some news on Toby, and she'd shared it with the rest of the class. She did wonder how the little boy was doing, and she was going to look into that when she had time. Her heart broke for the little family when she thought about all that had happened to them.

"We've moved." He asked her where they had moved to. "To the house that Brenin owns. We're going to be his house guests."

"Why? Did something happen to our old house?" She said that the rent had gone up again, and they couldn't afford it without her working more. "I don't want you to work more, Mom. I miss you so much now. Is Mr. Brenin going to be there all the time?"

"Yes, it's his house, so he'll be living there with us. You'll get to ride the bus when you go to school tomorrow or the next day. We'll have to call the school and put you on the route." She knew that he'd be excited about that more than anything and wasn't disappointed when he yelped for joy. "All the rules still have to work for us, or we'll have to move out. You understand why, don't you?"

"Yes, so I don't have a meltdown when things aren't right. That only happened the one time, Mom. I'm older now." Yes, he was older by a whole year now. She told him that the house was going to be taken care of, too. "I won't leave my toys out where they can get stepped on. Do you suppose that Mr. Brenin will want to play ball with me in the yard? I think that would be cool. Don't you?"

"Only if you remember that he has a job too and might not have time to play with you." He sounded so certain when he said he'd make time that she didn't have the heart to tell him anything different. "You're taking this move a lot better than I thought you would. Why is that?"

"I thought you were going to tell me that we had to live with Grandma. I don't like her very much." She said that wasn't nice and asked him what she'd done to him. "She wants me to tell her when you do things." She asked him what sort of things, but they were home now, and he was distracted by the new house. "Look how big it is."

He ran from room to room, and she let him. It was exciting to be living someplace new, and so she left him explore. But she was going to ask him about what sort of things Janice was having him tell on her about as soon as possible. She had an idea what was going on, but wasn't sure either that she wanted to know. Things were getting very bad concerning her mother-in-law.

Chapter 4

For the first time since moving into his new house, Brenin was looking forward to going home. There would be people there waiting on him, and he couldn't wait. As soon as he walked in the door, he knew something had happened, and he waited for Lisa to tell him what had happened rather than bombarding her with questions.

"Janice again." He simply nodded and looked at Davy. "He loves the house and can't wait until the pool is open again in the summer. He's had swimming lessons, but I don't know that I trust him being out there all alone."

"We'll all enjoy the pool come summer. I can't wait either. It was too cold when I bought the house to live in to use it, so I've been waiting too." He asked Davy how he liked his room. He told him excitedly, and that made him laugh a little. "Mom gave me the rules that we have to follow, so don't try to pull the wool over my eyes when we're here alone. All right?"

"Mom told me that you're going to be picking me up from school sometimes, too. I like that. Sometimes I'm the only boy in my class who only has his mom picking him up. Other kids have step-dads or something like an uncle to pick them up." He asked him if he had his homework done. "I have to do that as soon as I get home. Mom already went over the site words with me, too. I had to read at least five pages of my book, too. It's all done."

"Good to know. Also, tomorrow I'm picking you up after school, unless we can get the bus to bring you home. I don't know how much later you'll be, but you won't be getting home at the same time as before." He nodded and seemed distracted. "What's up, buddy? You all right with living here? I promise you that things will be better in the future. I'm going to take care of you and your mom."

"I know that. I was talking to my friend Parker, his new dad is a shifter too. Mom said you were a dragon, and everybody knows that about you. But Parker said that he's good to him and never gets mad at him about stuff." He said that was a good thing, right? "Yeah, it's all good, but I worry about mom. Grandma isn't going to be happy with her about living with you. She said that it's a sin for her to be dating anyone when she's had a husband already."

"Your grandma is wrong about that. And we'll be just sharing a house, nothing more. You understand that?" He shrugged and told him he thought that Mom would be happier about not working a lot. "I'm sure that she will be. It'll take some time for her to get used to working just one job, too. If that's what she wants. She doesn't have to work at all, but I know that she has to. I do as well. It stems from being so old and getting bored easily. I have to keep busy."

There was something still bothering him, he could tell, but he waited for him to tell him what it was. There was no point in pushing him into telling him. He wanted them to have a good relationship from the start, and pushing him wouldn't help that.

After dinner of hot dogs and fries, the three of them went over the rules for the house again. They weren't that hard to remember. It was mostly about after school and how homework had to be done right away. The rest were things like he had to eat all his dinner if he got seconds, and there were rules about bedtime, too. He didn't have to go to bed when he went to his room at eight o'clock, but he had to be asleep by nine. He thought that was a good rule to have. He didn't necessarily want to go to sleep as soon as he went to his room, either.

The rest were things like when he was with the little boy. He wasn't to take him out anywhere without having him buckled in. He had a booster seat that he was required to sit in, and since he didn't have one for his car, then he'd get one. Until then, they'd have to share.

He loved that the rules were just simple things that had to do with the safety of Davy. She had rules for herself, too, but he wasn't too upset about them. She wasn't going to do anything to his house without permission, and that she would not share a bed with him until she was ready. He knew that he wanted her, but he could live by her rules on that for as long as she needed. He didn't want to rush her into anything, and that applied to sex as well.

When he was ready for bed, he told Lisa that he'd see her in the morning. After locking up the house, he was about as exhausted as he'd been in a while. It was a good kind of being tired, like he'd worked hard at something and was tired from that instead of boredom. As soon as he plugged in his phone to charge after setting the alarm, he was ready for a good night's sleep. As soon as he turned out the light, he was out.

The next morning, he felt better than he had in previous mornings. He thought it had a lot to do with having someone in the house besides him. Once he made it to the kitchen, he was ready for something big to eat. As soon as he sat down, there was a huge plate of food set in front of him, and he was digging into it when Davy joined him in the kitchen.

"Will you adopt me?" He was startled by the question and told him that it would be up to his mom and him. "I've been a Manchester all my life, and I'd like to be a Savage now." He nearly laughed but caught himself just in time.

"You've worn that name well if you ask me. Why don't you want to be a Manchester anymore? You have to have a good reason." He nodded and played with his food as he seemed to be thinking about how to answer him. "Buddy, you can talk to me about anything. You know that, don't you? I'm here for you as much as I am your mom."

"I know that. You listen to me really well, too. But Grandma said that being a Manchester has responsibilities, and I'm only seven. I don't want to have to be responsible for making sure that the line is carried on. I don't even know what that means." He did laugh then and explained how he was supposed to marry someday and have a son to carry on the name. "I don't even like girls, much less want to be married to one." He sounded so shocked by the notion of marrying a girl that Brenin laughed hard.

"You'll change your mind about girls when you get a bit older. Right now, you're just a little boy, and that's who I'll love." He looked at him with serious eyes and asked if he loved him. "I do. I've not said that to your mother yet, but I love her as well. She's my heart and soul."

"That's mushy stuff." He agreed with him and got him going for school. "Mom usually drops me off at daycare when she has to work the early morning shift. This is nice, where I don't have to go there with the other littler kids. They think that it's cool that they get to ride the bus to school in the morning. I'm excited about being dropped off at this place. I love this house."

"I do now, too, since you and your mom live here. You never said how you liked your room. Is it up to standards for you?" He told him that he loved how big it was and that he had room to play there, too. "I guess it's good that you've moved in as well. I love the two of you being here."

"I love it too. And the pool. I had swimming lessons this past summer. Mom said if I do really good, then I can have a pool party on my birthday next time. That's why I had to have lessons. Some of the other kids would invite me to their pool parties, and I didn't know how to swim. Mom's really good at making sure I can fit in with everyone else." He told him that he fit into his life as well. "Good. I won't embarrass you or anything when we're out together. I don't mind getting hugs, either, but no kissing. You're a man, and I'm a little boy. People will think I'm some kind of pervert or something. I'm not sure what that means either, but I think it means that I'm weird."

He thought that was as good a description as any and didn't tell him anything different. He was going to have to ask Lisa if she told him the truth when he had questions, or if she fobbed him off until he was older. He had a feeling that she told him as much truth as he could handle for a kid, and that was the end of it. Just enough to satisfy him yet answer the questions truthfully. He could do that, too.

Dropping him off at school was fun. He knew just what to do when the teachers came out to help the kids get out of the cars. As soon as he was free to go on his way, he told Davy that he loved him and would see him after school. Just as he was leaving the lot, he got a call from the school.

"The bus will pick Davy up tomorrow. He'll have to have an adult with him when he rides to school, and once he's on the bus, then he'll be the responsibility of the bus driver. He'll be dropped off the same way. The driver won't allow him off the bus if there's no one there to pick him up. Understand?" He said that he did and would be there. "I don't know the times, but expect him around four o'clock. I'd be there a little earlier, just in case he's in the line to be dropped off earlier. The same with pick up. He'll be picked up anywhere between eight-thirty and a quarter to nine."

He was told to be there early, as they didn't know the route that well yet, so it might be earlier than mentioned. Brenin said he'd be there on time and would wait with Davy. After she repeated everything that she'd said to him, making sure that he knew what he was doing, he made a mental note to message Lisa the schedule so that she'd be aware of the bus pick up and drop off. With him there, she was going to be able to save money on the after-school daycare, too, he only just realized. He hoped that she'd not want to work so hard, but he couldn't blame her for needing to work. They were new to one another, and she was still figuring out if she could trust him or not. He was all right with that so long as she was giving him a chance. He thought that he could conquer the world so long as she trusted him not to hurt her.

Heading to work early, he decided that he was going to be ready for the day better than he had in a while. Sometimes it was difficult to get going in the morning, but today he felt like he had the energy to get all his work done and maybe get a jump on tomorrow's day. As he was getting his computer set up to check his emails, he heard from the school again.

"Mr. Savage? We tried to get in touch with Davy's mother, but she's not answering her phone. He's been hurt." He asked what had happened, already grabbing his coat to go to him. "He was in first period when he fell and hurt his knee. I don't believe that there is any cause for alarm, but we have a note on his file that we're to call his mother when he gets hurt, no matter what it is."

"I'll be right there." He was in his car when he

realized that he didn't know anything about Davy's doctors or if he was allergic to anything. He was going to need a list of things like that if he had to take him to the hospital for some reason. "I'll check him over and decide if he'll need to go to the hospital or not. His mother is working and can't be reached."

"I understand. Like I said, it's just a fall, and he's scraped up his knees, but we're to call no matter what happens to him." He told her that the same would still apply even though he was going to come in. "All right. But it seems like a waste of time to come in for a little boo-boo."

"I'll decide if it's a boo-boo or not, and I'd appreciate it if you would not comment on the way things are done between his family and his being hurt at school. It's my understanding that he'd been hurt before and was misdiagnosed when he had a broken bone." She apologized, and he didn't tell her it was all right. He only hoped that Davy was all right. He didn't want to have to explain to his mom how he'd been hurt on his watch.

~*~

"It's just a couple of scratches, so he'll be fine." She was glad to have had Brenin put on the list to call if she wasn't available. She'd never put Janice on the list as she didn't trust her to do the right thing. Now, after hearing all the things that she'd been hearing about her, she was glad that she'd never done it. She didn't trust her at all now. "He said that he was all right at school, so I left him there. He was very brave, too, when I went to see him. He's a great kid."

"I know he is, and thank you for doing just what I would have done." Brenin told her that it was his pleasure as he'd been able to leave work when needed. "I've given my two weeks' notice here. I'm going to find something that has more stable hours. I can't work morning and then close the same night. It's too hard on me. But I'm going to continue to grade papers for the high school. It pays well, and I can be home when I'm working."

"You do what you need to do. I'm here for you." He told her about the bus schedule, and she was happy that he'd taken it seriously about how he was going to be there early. "I think we'll have fun with just getting to know one another while waiting for the bus. Plus, he won't have to wait in the cold either when full winter comes along."

"I'm glad for that. I don't want him to get sick waiting for the bus to pick him up." After her break was over, she decided that she was going to have to find something during the hours that Davy went to school. If she found anything. She wasn't sure that she wanted to work anymore than she had to, and that made her nervous. She'd been a hard worker all her life, and just because Brenin said he could afford for her to be at home all the time didn't mean she was going to take him up on it. What if they ran out of money just as she was getting used to being at home all the time? She had thoughts like that, along with how much money it would take to be able to say that they'd never have to work again. That would be a great deal of money as far as she was to understand.

Getting home at one, she was happy to know that dinner would be ready at six. She and Davy tried to eat at that time every night, and she was happy that the schedule was going to be adhered to. That way, he had plenty of time to get his homework finished and to play in his room afterwards. He was a great kid, and she loved him with all her heart.

Brenin was being so nice to her that she wasn't sure when the other shoe would drop. It was terrible for her to think that all the time, she knew that, but she didn't want to be out in the cold when things went bust. Even with her living with him right now, it was something that she should have thought more about. What if he decided that she wasn't going to be his mate anymore? Then where would she be? Out in the cold for sure. Or worse yet, living with Janice.

Just as she was sitting down to dinner, her cell phone rang. Since she'd just been thinking about Janice and what she'd done to her, she decided to let it go to voicemail. Putting her phone on silent when she called right back, Lisa enjoyed her real meal in the house that she'd fallen in love with from the first moment that she saw it.

After dinner, they sat in the living room, and she pulled out her phone. There were fourteen messages and three voicemails. Listening to the voicemails first, she wanted to know why the house that she'd been living in was empty. As the messages went on, they were more demanding. The text messages were even worse. She must have been using the talk-to-text app because there were so many typos that she thought it was funny. Calling her back was something that she didn't want to do, but felt the need to clear the air.

"What do you mean by not calling me back right away? I was upset, and you know how I get when I'm upset." She said that she was having dinner and didn't use her phone during that time. "Well, you'd better be making sure that I can get in touch with you from now on. Where are you? I've been by the house, and it's empty of all your things."

"We had to move." She didn't feel the need to explain, so she didn't elaborate anymore than that. "Why were you coming by the house? You never come over without an invite."

"I've been trying to contact you all day. And why did you have to move? Did you lose one of your jobs?" She told her how the rent went up and that they had to find some place they could afford. "Without coming to me? I thought we had a deal. When you moved out because you couldn't afford it any longer, you would move in with me and let me babysit Davy for you."

"We didn't have any kind of arrangement like that at all. And I don't remember you saying anything about me moving in with you other than when David first died. Besides, I found a cheaper place, and we're doing just fine. I might even be able to quit one of my jobs." She asked her where she was living. "With a friend of mine. He's been really generous about giving up some of his space for Davy and I. It's working out better than I thought it would. He's already saving me money by being there so that Davy doesn't have to go to daycare after school."

So much for not telling her much, she thought with a sigh. While Janice talked about moving in with her, she ignored her for the most part. After knowing all that she did about the older woman, she wouldn't move in with her if that's all she had other than a cardboard box. She'd raised the rent on her place because she wanted them to move in with her. That was never going to happen.

"I have all this space. And don't think I didn't catch that you'd be living with some man, either.

You've had a husband, and you don't need another man in your life." She said for now they were just friends. "For now? What does that mean? I surely hope you're not thinking about living in sin with this man. As I said, you've had a husband, and that's all you need. You and Davy are going to be living with me, and that's final."

"I say what's final in our lives, not you. And I will not be living with you." Janice screamed so loudly that she had to pull the phone from her ear. "What is the matter with you? You're acting like you own me or something. Davy and I are doing just fine, and we don't need help from you. That's final."

Hanging up the phone made her feel good about the conversation. It wasn't going anywhere in the first place, and she didn't care for the conversation anyway. Janice was insane if she thought that she'd move in with her just because she'd raised the rent too high for her to afford anymore. All the other things that she'd done since her son had been killed were starting to make sense now. All of her moves had been for one thing: her and her son to move in with the woman so that she could keep an eye on her and Davy. Why? She didn't have a clue, but it wasn't going to happen.

"She's calling again." Picking up her phone, she put it on silent again and put it back on the table. Looking at Brenin, she thanked him for the information that he'd been able to get for her concerning Janice. "It was my pleasure. I just hope that she stays away now that you've moved out of the house. She could be a problem for Davy at school, too. Is she on the list to be able to pick him up?"

"No. In fact, for my own sanity, I said she was never to pick him up. I don't know why, but I always had a feeling that I'd never get him back if she were to get him. Don't ask me why, but it's just a feeling that I've had since he was little." He thought that was as good a reason as any. "Why do you suppose she wants us to live with her? I have my own ideas, so she can keep an eye on me, but what do you think?"

"I believe you have the right of it. Not only that, but from some of the things that Davy said that she's said to him, I think she won't care for the fact that you and I would be getting married someday soon. Speaking of which, do you have any idea what sort of wedding you want? I was thinking that we just have it filed at the courthouse, but that's entirely up to you." She said she was fine with that, so long as Davy could be there when they exchanged rings. "I have one for you. It was given to me in the estate that was my great-grandma's. She said that she wore it for a while but never liked it. If you don't care for it, we can get you something else. I think that it's beautiful." He showed her the ring.

"Oh my, that is lovely. Why didn't she care for it?" He told her and then explained that grandda had gotten it in an estate sale once. "I love it. It's the perfect ring that I would have picked out for myself. Just give it to me when Davy's around, and we'll be fine with getting married. I don't want a big ceremony or anything like that."

"Good. Then I'll have one of the faeries file it away in the books in the courthouse, and that'll be finished. You'll be Mrs. Lisa Savage." He told her what Davy had said about being a Manchester. "I think that I'd love to have him named Savage for all the same reasons. He's a great kid, and I would love to adopt him."

"The added bonus will be that it pisses Janice off." She laughed, then looked at Brenin. "I'm sorry. That wasn't right to make a joke about. I'm sorry about that."

"It's all fine, and right now I agree with you. She's done enough harm to the two of you since David passed that it only stands to reason that you'd want to get back at her." Lisa said that she really wanted to get back at her for all the times she had to choose between food or rent. "I'm just happy you don't have to make decisions like that again. There will never be a time when you have to make choices like that again."

"Thank you for that." She sat on the couch for

a few more minutes and then asked him about them getting married. "I think we should do it soon. I don't like the fact that Davy is being told one thing and we're doing the opposite. He needs to have a stable home. I do as well, and the only way that I can think that we can do that is to get married. But nothing else changes. I'm not ready to have sex with you as yet. I'm still fumbling around about living here."

"I understand, and nothing will happen until you're ready. Being married will make it so that when I put your name on things like deeds to homes that I own, it'll be legal. Also, before I forget, you need to go to the bank to sign off on a few things. I've put you on my checking account and also my savings. There is quite a bit of money in both accounts, so don't not use it when you need to." She nodded, but she wasn't sure that she understood. "I have a great deal of money, Lisa. You don't ever have to worry about money again, so long as we're together, and that's going to be a long time."

"You said that I was immortal like you. Is Davy as well?" He explained how he would grow up to be about twenty before he would stop aging altogether. Then he would live a full life. "But he can still be hurt, correct? Like his knees being scraped up?"

"Yes, he can be hurt, but he'll heal faster. The both of you will. Unlike a human, he'll be able to sustain more injuries to his body, just like you will, and walk away from it. You only have to be careful of having your head removed, and I don't see that happening to anyone around here. It's difficult to do, and the only way I can have my head removed is as my human self. But even then it's not so easy." She asked if it was because he could shift into his dragon. "Yes. I can better fight if I'm my dragon. You'll have to see him sometime. Davy has asked to see him as well."

"I'd like that." When she glanced at her phone, he could tell she was upset about Janice. The woman was going to be dangerous if he didn't miss his bet. While he didn't know what she'd do, he was sure that it wasn't going to be nice. The woman had a real hard on for having them live with her, and he didn't understand it other than what Lisa had said; it was so that she could keep an eye on her. Why? He didn't know, but he'd bet before too much longer he'd find out.

Chapter 5

Lisa spent most of her morning wrapping silverware for work. She was bored out of her mind, but knew that if anyone came in for lunch, they'd be ready for them. When Shanda sat down beside her, she knew that she wouldn't say much to her. Shanda had been a snitch for Janice before. And she knew that was how she'd found out that she'd given her notice at work. Janice wasn't thrilled about her not working either.

"Where are you living now?" She nearly laughed, but didn't. She usually enjoyed it when someone was right to the point, but not today. "I heard that you moved out in the middle of the night. That's so you didn't have to pay rent."

"I moved into something cheaper. And I'm living with a friend of mine so that I can afford to not have to work so hard." She asked her where she was living again. "Not far from here. It's in a good neighborhood, too. I love it."

"You still never said where you were living. Or is that a big secret?" She asked her why it was important to her that she tell her. "I just want to know in case I ever want to come by or something. No big deal if you don't want to tell me."

"I don't. I hope that's all right. Besides, you never came by to see me at my other home. Why would you be coming around there?" She shrugged, and Lisa went back to wrapping the silverware that had just come out of the kitchen. "I'm betting it won't be busy tonight either. It's turned cold, and no one wants to venture out into the weather. I know that once I get home, I'm going to enjoy having my car in the garage and not out in the weather too."

They talked a bit more, Shanda still trying to get her address from her in other ways. Did she have to travel long to get to work? What was Davy doing about daycare? Was he still going? She didn't answer any questions about her personal life and thought that she'd done fine in shutting her down. But just like Janice, she was on a mission to get the information, and there was no stopping her, apparently. Finally, she told her that she wasn't going to talk to her anymore if she didn't stop asking personal questions, and she went away with a huff. Good. One less thing she had to worry about. Now all she had to do was make sure that she wasn't going to be followed home. She wouldn't put anything past either one of them in getting the address that way.

At four o'clock, she was ready to go home. The weather had gotten nastier than it had been this morning, and she wasn't looking forward to driving home in it. As soon as she got on the road, she noticed that there were no trucks out cleaning the road of the snow and wondered if Davy would have school tomorrow. Living in a rural area meant that back roads were gotten to last if ever, and there was no way the buses would be able to get through them, not the way they looked now.

It took her an hour to get home from a fifteen-minute drive, which was usually how long it took her. Getting in the house, she was greeted by Davy and Brenin waiting for her. Giving her hot chocolate and cookies was the perfect end to the day she'd had. Getting a kick out of Shanda and her questions, she laughed with Brenin about it, and Davy thought it was funny too.

"They said that you're going to have to fill out paperwork at school for my new address and stuff. They also want to make sure that my insurance hasn't changed." She said she'd take care of it in the morning. "I don't think we're going to have school. My bus driver said the roads were too bad tonight, driving home. I wonder if we'll miss too much school."

"The weather is supposed to get better over the next several days. This snowstorm came out of nowhere, I guess." She didn't know much about the weather but relied on the app on her phone to tell her what she needed to know. "I guess we'll have to get used to this all together now instead of just you and me getting used to it. Right?"

"The bus ride was fantastic. I got to sit where I wanted, and I sat with my friend from school. The bus goes to the daycare, too, where I was." Brenin asked if he'd known not to get off. "I wasn't sure. But the bus driver knew. Her name is Ms. Sally. She didn't wreck us or anything on the way home tonight."

"That's good." She was glad that he was getting to ride the bus. It would be a good way for him to be able to socialize with other kids, too, who were younger and older than him. "I guess we'll have to worry about school in the morning together. I'm not working until noon lunchtime."

After dinner, they sat in the living room and talked. Davy was playing quietly with his trucks when Brenin pulled out the ring and asked her to marry him. He even had a gift for Davy, another truck like the one he was playing with, and he asked him if he'd be his boy. Of course, it was a big hit, and she was glad that Brenin had thought about him. It was nearly eight o'clock when they called school off for tomorrow, and Davy was happy with that. He said he'd miss riding the bus, but he was all right with it since she'd be home in the morning with him.

When Davy went to his room, she and Brenin

watched the television. She wasn't used to having free time to watch it, so she didn't have any idea what sort of programs to watch. Finally, they turned it off in favor of the quiet, and she liked that even better. At ten after ten, she was headed to bed, and Brenin said he'd be up for a while. He had some work to be done on the computer. After telling him goodnight, she headed to the bedroom that she'd been using and got ready for bed.

Almost like her body energized, she couldn't sleep as soon as she got into the bed. Her mind was working on issues that had never been one before, and she worried about Janice. She wondered, not for the first time, whether she would try to take Davy from her, and that upset her. There had to be a good reason why she was doing the things that she was doing to her and her son, but she couldn't for the life of her figure out what it would be. The one thought that kept going through her mind was that she wasn't going to go away nicely and that someone was going to get hurt. She could only think that she hoped it wasn't Davy, as he'd had enough trauma in his life for a seven-year-old kid.

Finally getting up, she got her laptop and started looking for jobs. She wasn't sure that she wanted one, but it didn't hurt her to look. There was an advertisement for a waitress position where she worked, and she wondered if anyone would apply, but she skipped over that one in favor of something that would be during the day. Finding nothing, she did a search on Janice just through the search engine and read everything with her name in it.

She'd not known that Janice had worked before she'd met David. He only called her a housewife, and when she pulled up David Senior's death notice, she'd read where she'd been working for a local attorney's office in Zanesville. While it didn't say what she did for them, she had retired after thirty years and with good standing. Also, it told how she'd been thought of by the office for the loss of her husband.

Lisa had never met David Senior before marrying David. He'd been gone only a few years when they started dating, and that was all she knew about him from what he'd said about his dad. She did know that Davy had been named for the two of them, and he was the third David Manchester. It didn't bother her at all that there would be no more Manchester's from the family line. She thought that three had been plenty. Of course, that would depend on Brenin adopting Davy and giving him his last name.

Getting to work the next afternoon wasn't as difficult as it had been in getting home the night before. All the main streets were cleared off. Even the parking lot at work had been gone over, so she was able to find herself a good parking place there, too. As soon as she got into the restaurant, she knew that the shit was about to hit the fan. Janice and Shanda were huddled together in a booth with their heads together. Whatever was going on, it wasn't going to bode well for her.

"There you are. I thought you'd not be coming in today since there was no school." She told Shanda that she was on the schedule and would work so long as she could get to work. "I was just talking to Janice here, and she doesn't know where you live either. We've come to the conclusion that it must not be a very good place if you're keeping it from everyone. Why don't you tell us where you're living?" Tired of the games, she said it wasn't any of their business. "See? I told you that she'd not give it to you. She's not been talking about a lot of things going on in her life."

"As I said, it's none of your business." She went to clock in and was dismayed when they followed her back to the time clock. "Why do you care anyway? It's not like you owned the house that I was living in, did you? I mean, that would just be cruel of you to raise my rent when you knew we were struggling."

If she hadn't been looking right at Janice when she said that, she would have missed her face turning an angry shade of red. Blustering about how she was on a fixed income and could barely afford her own house payment, much less one on a house that she was renting, Lisa decided that she'd had enough. She told her that she knew she owned the house and shouldn't have been charging so much, as she was related to her.

"You're not related to me at all since you asked. Davy is my grandson, and that's as far as I'm going to allow you around me. All this intrigue is for the birds. Tell me where you live, or I'll have to call the police on you. You've taken my grandson away from me, and I'm not going to tolerate it." She snorted, thinking that was the craziest thing she'd ever heard.

Instead of getting into it with her, she went to the tables to make sure they were ready for the afternoon crowd. Or whoever might come in needing a good meal. Ignoring the two of them for things to keep her mind occupied, Lisa made sure that the tables were set that were usually used for dinner when five o'clock rolled around. It wasn't until Shanda grabbed her arm and jerked her around that she got pissed off.

"What do you think you're doing? Unhand me." Shanda did let her go, but she laughed while she was at it. "The two of you are insane. I'm not going to tell you where I live now even if you did call the police."

The slap to her face was unexpected and painful. Janice had hit her and was drawing back to no doubt hit her again when Mr. Weaver, the owner of the restaurant, stepped in. He asked what was going on and if Lisa needed help. She said that she'd been hurt by Janice and that she didn't know why.

"I've called the police. See what they have to say about this." Tasting blood on her lip, she let it go. If she had to, she'd press charges against Janice so that she'd be arrested. Assault wasn't something that she had hoped would happen, but she was glad that she wasn't healing right away. "You'll have to give me your address now."

The look on her face was priceless. She looked as if she'd won. Lisa didn't know how it was going to work with the police coming by, but she was willing to bet that they'd tell her that she didn't need to give up her address. It was personal, not something that everyone needed. She waited on a table when a couple came in just to prove that she wasn't upset about it.

"Hello, Lisa." She turned around when she heard Brenin behind her and was freaked out a little that he wasn't around. *"It's Brenin. I should have explained earlier that we could talk to one another like this, but I forgot. Just think of what you want to say, and I'll hear you. No one else needs to know that we're talking."*

"This is so cool." She could feel his humor, and that made her smile. After taking her table their drinks, she told him what was going on at work. *"I don't know what the police are going to say, but I'm waiting for them to come here."*

"They won't do anything other than arrest them both if you press charges for assault. That's entirely up to you. But I'd do it so that the next time she thinks hitting you is all right, she'll think about the consequences." She told him that had been her plan, but she was worried about pissing her off more. *"It's been known that pissed-off people make big mistakes. You just do what you want, and I'll be behind you one hundred percent. So will the department. They're good friends of mine and will do it for you just because they know me. But as I said, you do what you want."*

"I'm pressing charges. I don't need to be beaten up, even for a little bit, because she doesn't know where I live." He said it would be easy enough for her to follow her home. *"That's what I thought too. Maybe she's beneath that sort of thing."*

She told him about what she'd said about the house, and he laughed again. When the police arrived, she waited until Janice and Shanda told their side of the story before Mr. Weaver said he'd seen the whole thing. Asking if she wanted to press charges, Janice said no, but she said yes, she wanted to. The two of them were arrested on assault charges and taken away. She felt so good that she said that she could work until closing for Shanda, who was going to miss her shift. Mr. Weaver said they'd be all right and laughed with her. It was good that she'd made friends with him when she'd been hired.

~*~

Janice couldn't believe that she'd been arrested. She was an upstanding person of the community and didn't care for being treated like a common criminal. The worst part was that she still didn't know where Lisa was living, and that burned her toast. She had to know where she was living so that she could serve her with papers about her being a bad parent. Who moved into someone else's home when she'd had a perfectly good one living with her? It just wasn't right.

No matter what she did to the woman, she would always bounce back on her feet like nothing happened. She was tired of all this shit going on and was going to have to take steps to get the boy from her. Davy should have been with her from birth, and she nearly had her son convinced when he'd gotten himself killed.

For as much as she wanted to blame that on Lisa, too, there was no way to do it. David had been in the wrong place at the wrong time, they'd told her, and had been killed. She was never going to get over his death, and she didn't understand why Lisa had. It wasn't right that she was moving on with her life when she was still grieving about her only child.

Davy living with her would help; she just knew that. He was upset with her now, not wanting to cuddle any time she wanted, but he'd get over that soon enough. A couple of little swats to his ass would have him doing as he was told. Lisa never spanked Davy, and she didn't understand that either. If they had moved in with her when she wanted, he'd be trained to be her grandson the way that she wanted, and that would have been perfect. As it was now, he was a spoiled little brat who thought that hugging her was too mushy. Whatever the hell that was supposed to mean.

"You're going to be in here until Thursday. That's when the judge comes through to see about pretrials." She said that she wanted out now to set her bail. "There is no bail until you see the judge. Then, after that, you'll have to have someone bring you the money. We don't take credit cards, only cash."

"That's ridiculous. Even the library takes credit cards for late fees." He told her that they weren't the library. "No, I doubt very much you even know what that is. Have you even graduated from high school? Good lord, it's like talking to a wall with all of you around here. I'm glad that I've had no use for you before now. It's your fault that my son was killed, I'm betting."

"I knew David. He was a good man. And a better friend to all those who knew him." She wanted to lash out at him, thinking that her son would lower himself to be friends with the likes of him. Instead of saying anything, she went to sit on the cot. "You have one phone call to make, and then they'll ask you if you have an attorney. If so, you'd best be calling him instead of anyone else. We won't be making phone calls on your behalf."

"You'll do as you're told, and I won't have it any other way. I pay my taxes, and I know that I pay your salary too. When I want something, you're to jump to get it." He simply walked away from her, and she wasn't going to lower herself to calling him back. "Damned police. I have no idea to this day why my son thought that it would be good for him to be a lowlife cop."

It was a good hour before they came to tell her she could make a phone call. Something about having a payphone was all she was able to use, and she asked them how she was supposed to make that work when she had a perfectly good cell phone that had all her numbers stored in it. They, in the end, let her use her phone, but they didn't leave her alone with it. She could make one phone call, and then she'd get it taken from her again. Damn it all to hell. She shouldn't have been arrested in the first place, and now here she was in jail for no other reason than she had a stupid daughter-in-law.

It had occurred to her over the last several

months that she should just have Lisa killed. It would solve all her problems, and she'd have her grandson, too. It was beginning to look like she was going to have to do something like that before it was all over, and she didn't care for it. Getting caught was her biggest fear. Or having Davy find out that she'd done it was something else. He'd never forgive her for having his stupid mother killed, so she wasn't thinking about that too much right now. It wasn't that she didn't think about it, but she knew that if it came down to it, she could afford the best there was to do the job. No more pussyfooting around, either. But not just yet.

After calling her attorney, she decided to make another call. But before she could get the phone to work, it was snatched from her like she didn't have things to get done. Screaming at the officer when he stood over her, smiling, she wanted to hit him right in the face. But hitting someone again, especially a police officer, would get her into more trouble than she was in right now. Besides, they'd all pay before she was finished with them, and she couldn't wait until they got their comeuppance.

Janice didn't think of herself as a terrible person. Entitled, yes, but then why wouldn't she be? She was just one who liked things to go her way. And her way was the only way there was, she thought with a grin. She'd been getting her way since before she'd been in high school, and she liked it. Getting her husband to marry her was the greatest accomplishment that she'd ever made. Now, when she got her grandson to live with her, preferably without his mother, then she'd be two for two in getting what she wanted.

Shanda was just down the hall from her, but she'd served her purpose, so she wanted nothing more to do with her. As she kept yelling for her to get her out, too, she ignored her in favor of making plans about what she was going to do when Davy lived with her.

Now that he was getting older, she decided that she was going to call him David. Davy sounded like a baby's name, and she didn't want people to think that she was raising him to be anything but a man. A better man than her husband and son had been for sure.

Dinner was nothing she would have served her dog had she had one. It was some kind of sandwich with a bag of chips. She was told that since she'd been so late coming in, they'd not been prepared for her, so her next meals would be better. It certainly couldn't get any worse than what they expected her to eat tonight.

Eating the cake over the meal, she decided that someday she was going to run this town, and the police station would be the first to go. There was very little use for it, and she didn't think that her taxes should go for something so lame as a one-light town having a stationhouse.

They announced that the lights would be out at ten. She wasn't going to have that, as she stayed up late when she was at home. It was nothing for her to get to bed around the time that the sun was coming up. They'd just have to make an exception for her since she wasn't going to mess up her schedule just because they thought that lights out meant that she was tired and would be going to bed. Not that she'd be able to sleep on the little bed that she'd had. Janice wondered what she'd have to do to get herself a better bed while she was in jail. Certainly, nothing more than giving out money to the right people. The only thing was, she didn't think that there were any right people in this place to do anything she wanted. They came to get her tray, and she decided then to have a word with someone about the conditions she was forced to endure.

"What do I have to do to get a better bed? Not to mention better meals. I shouldn't be in here at all, much less living like the others do." He said that she had what she got, and that was nothing more than the other inmates had. "But I shouldn't be here at all. All I did was bloody her lip. It's not like she needed stitches or anything. I guess next time I'll have to knock her around more so that I can get what I want."

Thinking about what she said, she knew the reason why he was looking at her, confused. But she wasn't going to admit to anything but let him stew about it. After he left her, telling her that lights out was going to be in an hour, she tried to get him to come back so that she could tell him how much that wasn't going to work for her. The stupid fool just walked away, and she felt her temper getting the better of her.

"You dumb mother fucker, you heard me. If you turn out the lights in an hour, I'm going to have you arrested." Yes, she thought that had worked out so well for her before. "I want you to leave my lights on until I'm ready to have them turned off. I know my rights. You'll do as I say or I'll stop paying my taxes. Then where will you be?"

"Employed," he yelled back at her, and she could almost see red; her temper was so out of control. "You have a nice night now."

There was no way that she was going to put up with this. She had paid her taxes when they came due, and she thought that should give her special privileges. Janice thought that when you paid as much as she did in taxes every year, it should come with a get out of jail free card. She didn't remember the name of the game that had that in it, but she thought that it should be the law no matter what.

When the lights went out, she was plunged into darkness. It had been getting nighttime earlier all the time, and with the sun already gone down, there wasn't even a flicker of stars that shone into her room. Not that she had a window or anything, but she should have been given more time. As it was now, she had to fumble around in the dark to get her bed made. They apparently couldn't even be bothered to make her bed for her.

The darkness had never been her friend. She had too many thoughts going around in her head to justify going to sleep. All she could think about was her baby boy and how he'd left her too soon. Crying to herself, she felt her heart break whenever she thought about how young he'd been when he'd left her behind.

She must have dozed off because when the lights came on, she was awakened by it. Wanting to sleep more now that the lights were on, she didn't get up when her breakfast was brought to her. But the delicious smells had her getting up to see what was under the domed food that was there.

Even the coffee was good. There had been two scrambled eggs done perfectly. Bacon and sausage links. The hashbrowns were just the way she liked them, with just enough crisps on them to make them crunch in her mouth. The toast was still warm, and the butter to put on it was just as soft as the toast was crunchy. Eating every bit of her meal, she almost couldn't wait until lunch. It wouldn't be as good, she told herself, but she would have to wait. As soon as they came for her tray, they told her that she had a visitor. It was her attorney. The first thing she told him was that she wanted out of here.

"Since you hit someone in a public setting, you'll have to wait your turn with the judge. I can't believe I have to tell you this after all this time. You should never do anything where there might be witnesses." She liked this man; he spoke to her like she liked. Telling her things that would keep her out of jail wasn't very helpful now, but she knew he'd get her out of here. "As it stands right now, the young woman you hit had to have three stitches. That doesn't sound like much, but when you factor in that you were going to hit her again—with witnesses, I might add—then that's going to get you some jail time. What were you thinking?"

"I was thinking that I'd heard enough of her mouth running." He just tsked at her. "What are you finding out about me getting my grandson from his mother? Have you found out anything that I can use against her in the court of law? I want to do this legally, but I'm not opposed to doing things the hard way if necessary."

"She's married. As of this morning, she and one of the Savage men are married. He's also making it so that he's going to adopt the little boy. You're going to be shit out of luck going up against them. They have all the money." She asked if that was true that they were dragons. "I've heard that too. But I don't think it makes any difference to the judge. He's a shifter too."

"Is there anyone around that cares that she's raising my grandson to be a pussy? I want him in my home by the end of the month. If you can't do it, then find me someone who will do as I want." He said that they were being recorded. "I don't care. I want her dead if I can't have what I want. And dead would be better than not. She won't be coming back to haunt me then."

They talked about her options, which weren't all that many. As he was getting ready to leave, he told her that he'd make sure to keep someone on her at all times. Then he told her that it was going to be difficult for her to get the boy if he adopted him. He'd be just one more person in line to get him if anything happened to his mother.

"What's this world coming to if a woman can't raise her grandson when the mother is such a slut." She didn't have any idea if she was or not, but it sounded good. As soon as she was taken back to her cell, she remembered that she should have asked him to get her a phone. It was the least he could do for her since she was paying him so much an hour to get her out of situations like this one.

Chapter 6

The restaurant wasn't busy at all for the next several days. She had a total of three customers on Monday and fewer than that on Tuesday. She was glad that she was leaving the place on Saturday because business wasn't going to be there, so there would be no tips. And the tips were what she paid for groceries with.

Living in the big house with Brenin and Davy was fun. She loved that they could spread out in the large rooms, and sitting in front of the fireplace was one of her all-time favorite things to do. It was warm and pretty, and when she was alone in the house, she would take a nap like she was some kind of diva.

Grading papers in the dining room at the table, she would finish them up sooner than before. She thought it was because she had so much room to spread out there, too, but didn't know. As soon as she was finished with one stack of papers, she started on the next one. It paid better than the waitressing job, and she didn't have to go to work to get it done. Not to mention, she didn't have to deal with Shanda or Janice when they showed up.

The knock at the front door startled her out of

her rhythm. She supposed she could have gotten up and answered it, but he had staff for that, and she wouldn't know what to do with someone coming by for him anyway. Turns out it was for her. It was the other women in the family. They'd come by to take her to lunch. Since she didn't have any excuses not to go, they bullied her into going with them. Davy wanted to stay home as he'd had no school this morning either, and there were plenty of people around the house to make sure that he didn't get into anything. She was out the door by twelve-thirty.

They were headed to the place she worked, and she thought that was a good thing. The place could use the business, and she thought it might be fun to be on the receiving end of being waited on. As soon as they were all seated around the largest table they had, the staff didn't seem to recognize her at all. Just as well. She'd never come into the place in anything but a uniform, so that was more than likely why they didn't know her.

Lunch was enjoyable. She got the lunch special of salad and tuna. The others got burgers and fries with milkshakes. It was a rare treat for her to be in the place when there were a lot of patrons, and she was happy for Mr. Weaver and the fact that she was helping in a way to keep him open. There had been talk about him closing down in the summer. She hoped that wasn't true. She loved the old place.

After lunch, they pulled out pads of paper and began working on projects. They all seemed to understand that she wasn't a part of that, so they'd pull her in for conversation whenever they could. Handed a pad of paper and a pen, she was making notes on things that she might be interested in helping with. Like the fall round-up at the school they had yearly. She also learned about the local pack and how they were taking students to study with them coming in spring. Skye turned to look at her with a smile on her face.

"I have a son, too. His name is Trevor. He's not really my son but a good friend that needed my help when we were hiding out from some very bad people." She told her how he'd come to be orphaned one day when he'd been just an infant, when the Connors—an older couple who had killed his parents for him—had taken him away and raised them as their own. He'd escaped, and the two of them had kept on the run together. "Kings and I adopted him just a few months ago. He's Trevor Savage now."

"That's what Brenin wants to do with Davy. I'm all right with that. It'll be one more hurdle for Janice to have to go through in her making it so she can get him." It was Kaida who asked why she wanted him. "I honestly don't know. She wants us to live with her so that she has more access to Davy. He doesn't care for her overly much. She's mad at him because he's not willing to spend the night with her anymore. And as crazy as she's been acting of late, I don't want him there either."

"The men will make sure that he's safe. When they tell you that, believe them. They have the resources, too, to make sure that you're both safe, too." She said that she was having a hard time realizing that everything that Brenin said to her was the truth. "Yes, they can't lie to you either. That's the best thing ever. They'll be there for you forever. And not just as a husband, but they become your best friend in everything you do, too. Did he tell you that you could shift? I've been doing it for over a week now, and it feels just like Kings said it does. Like you've got a whole new life." They both laughed.

"I just want to get this over with concerning Janice and Shanda. Shanda is just a pawn for Janice, but she's been so annoying. I'm finished working here as of tomorrow, but I'm going to help them out when they need it. I loved working here." Raven told her how she was going to school full-time to become an attorney. "That's wonderful. I had thought about going back to school to finish up my degree, but with Davy around needing me all the time, I've not been able to settle into one thing yet."

They talked around the table. She liked Raven best of all. She told her how she'd come to be with Cassian, Brenin's brother.

"It was my last day to work at a fast food place, and the manager wanted me to stay over and cover for him while he took a two-hour lunch. I'd already clocked out and didn't want to do it in the first place. He beat me up and broke bones. It was a month before I could get around on my own. Of course, Cassian could have healed me, but since the police were involved, he didn't. He did take away the pain, but not the wounds. I love him so much for doing what he did for me. My manager is in prison right now. He tried to tell the judge that I needed to be made to go with him to work so that he could knock me around. That was so that he'd not hit anyone else. And I was supposed to be all right with that." She said he sounded like a loon. "You have no idea. He really thought that since I was too poor being married to Cassian, I should be willing to do whatever was needed of me to make the world safe from his tempers. I'm glad he's gone. I've not had any more nightmares since then."

They each had similar stories about having someone in their lives who wanted more than they had to give. It was always the men who saved them, too. She wondered what Brenin would do to Janice if given the chance. She'd bet that he'd kill her and be done with her. She thought that they'd have that for plan 'B' and not kill her right away. The woman was off, but not to the point where she killed her yet. But if she hurt her son, then all bets were off, and she'd do the job herself. There was no way she was going to allow her to hurt her only child.

When they were finished for the day, she made her way back to the house by walking. It had turned into a warmer day than it had been recently, so she was happy to be able to enjoy the warmth. Davy would have school tomorrow, she'd bet, and was looking forward to him having a good day at school. It wore him out, going to school, and since he'd been off for the last two days, he wasn't burning off as much energy, so he was restless.

"I've been thinking about my friend Toby." She asked him what he'd been thinking about. "I want to go and see him. If his mommy doesn't care. We are best friends, and I miss him a great deal."

"We'll have to see what his mom says. He might not be much better and won't feel like company." He assured her that he'd want to have him there. "We'll just wait and see. I'll call her after supper and see what she has to say. All right?"

"All right. But he'll want to see me. I'm his bestest friend in the whole wide world, and we have to be together." He didn't go back to his room right away, and she waited. He would have what he wanted to say all worked out in his head before he spoke to her again. "Mommy, what happened to the boy who hurt him? He used to hurt me too, but I've not seen him at school for a long time. Do you think they put him in jail?"

"I'll ask her when I talk to her. I know nothing about the other boy other than his name is Tommy. Perhaps I can do some research on him to see what he's been up to." He seemed satisfied with that, and she hugged him. "There might not be much to find out since I don't have his last name. Did you ever remember it?"

"No. Everyone just called him Tommy." He started away but came back. "I'm afraid of him, just so you know. He used to beat on me too, but I never cried. He liked it when we cried when he hurt us."

After they ate together, she called Toby's mom. She said that Toby was awake now and sitting up, but he wasn't any better with the scars that were on his face and arms. She also told her that Tommy's parents were going to have to pay the hospital bill as she'd gotten an attorney.

"I can't afford this on my own. So I found an attorney to work with me, and he said that he'd make him pay the bills. I've lost my job because I've not been able to go to work." She said she was sorry. "Not as sorry as the family will be when my attorney gets through with them. He said that when it's all done and over, I shouldn't have to worry about anything. Toby is going to need extra surgeries to put his little face back together. As it is right now, he has over a hundred stitches in just his scalp." When she cried, Lisa told her how sorry she was. She also worried that Davy coming to see her son might not be such a good idea. "He looks so bad. And he cries a great deal from the pain that he's in. I would worry that Davy would have nightmares about how badly he looks."

"I'll tell him that we have to wait for another time to go and see him. Do you need anything? I can come by and sit with you if you'd like that. I'm not working as hard right now and would love to come by and sit down with you." She said that was nice, but she didn't want her to have nightmares either. It worried her that she'd said that several times now, and she worried about what the little boy looked like. And whether or not she was having her own nightmares. Lisa thought that she would.

Talking to Davy, he seemed to understand. He promised her that he'd not have any nightmares about the other little boy, then asked her what that meant. After explaining why he might not want to see him, he seemed to be upset that he was hurting so badly, but knew that he would abide by his mom's rules.

While Davy was reading his book that night,

he told her that he was going to be a doctor when he grew up. She thought that was the perfect thing to be, but he had a long time to decide. He told her that he wanted to be a doctor so that other little boys didn't have to suffer like his friend was. And having him as a doctor would solve all that. She hugged him tightly that night before putting him to bed, and it seemed as if they both needed it. She found Brenin in his office with his computer gone blank. He had his head back and was napping, so she didn't bother him.

Instead, she went up to bed to read more in her book and try to get an early start on the morning. She knew that she had to work the breakfast crowd in the morning and was both looking forward to it and not. It would be busy, but the tips would be terrible. It was her last day anyway, so she was hoping for a good day.

When her alarm went off, she didn't know where she was for a few minutes, so she laid in the bed looking around. When she figured out she was at Brenin's house and that Davy needed to be getting up for school, she hopped out of bed and got her shower. Getting Davy up was difficult; he wasn't a morning person, and getting him going was difficult. Since she had to be to work by six-thirty, she let Brenin deal with him and take him to the bus stop. It was nice to have someone help out when things were like this, and she was glad that Brenin seemed to enjoy it so much.

~*~

Brenin was going to be in the courtroom this morning for the hearing about Janice and Shanda. Shanda was already bitching about having to miss work and losing her job. Janice seemed to be in a good mood, but he knew that could just be a façade that she was carrying to fool the judge. He was careful around her table but sat up close enough that he could hear what was being said by all parties. When her name was called, he just knew she was going to be trouble.

"I want out of jail. I've been saying this since I was arrested, that there was no need for me to be put in jail. I only slapped the stupid woman the one time, and apparently that's against the law. All she had to do was move in with me, and that would have been the end of her troubles with her rent being due." The judge asked if she knew that she'd gotten stitches. "Three. Like that's anything to be bragging about. I've had worse cuts on my legs and didn't do anything about them. She's just milking the system."

"Be that as it may, you did hit her without provocation from her. Also, and this is something that I tell all my bullies, she's not going to be hit again, or you'll be right back here under worse circumstances. Do I make myself clear?" Janice said that she'd heard him. "What was the reason that you hit her in the first place? I heard you say something about her moving in with you. Perhaps she's smart in not wanting to live with you if you're going to go around hitting her for no reason."

"I owned the house that she was renting from me. I raised the rent so much that she'd have no choice but to move in with me so that I could help her raise my grandson. But she moved in with some man and is living there in sin with him, so that I can't see him. She won't even tell me where she's living. What kind of person does that to their mother-in-law? I wanted her to be beholden to me, and she's moved on without me. Ungrateful is what she is. I should be raising my grandson on my own for what she's been up to with that other person."

"I'm to understand that they're married." Brenin was never so glad to have something filed for himself as he was the marriage license that the faeries had put away for him. "So her living in sin isn't going to cut it. Also, there is an application for Mr. Savage to adopt the young lad as his own. I don't see anywhere on the paperwork where she had to have permission to do anything like moving in with you. She sounds to me like she's getting her life in order."

"She's moved on without so much as a thought to my feelings." The judge asked her why her feelings should come into play at all. "I'm her…haven't you been listening to me? I said she can't move on because my son was her husband. She had her chance at happiness, and now that's over. She should be living with me so that I can help her raise her son to be a good man. I don't believe for a moment that she has any idea what she's doing."

"Apparently, she has her own ideas when it comes to living with you. And she sounds to me like—you there? Are you a Savage?" He stood up and introduced himself to the room. "Brenin. You married this young woman. Does she seem like she needs help raising her son? I do believe that I married someone with that name recently. Anyway, does your wife seem like she needs to have Mrs. Manchester around her all the time to help with the raising of the child? I also have your application to adopt the boy, too. I'll go over it when we have a break."

"Lisa is doing an excellent job raising her son. She makes sure that he eats well and is in bed on time. His homework is always finished before dinner. She's a good mother to him and a better wife to me." The judge asked Janice why she thought she could do better. "I believe that Mrs. Manchester will stop at nothing to get her grandson to live with her. He doesn't even much care for her either."

"You shut your trap. I'll deal with you when I'm finished here. I'll not have you saying a bad word about me. I pay my taxes and should have things done my way." She turned to the judge before speaking again. "He'll be better off dead than living with the slut. I don't believe for a moment that she's married. It would be just like her to say something like that to have people believe that it's true. I want her and that grandson of mine living with me and not out and about like she's working the streets. You make that happen, and I'll be beholden to you for the rest of your term. If not…well, we'll just have to see how things turn out, won't we?"

"Are you threatening me, Mrs. Manchester? I'll have you know that's a stiff penalty for you to be messing with." She said that her taxes pay his salary and that he should be nicer to the people who pay the most. "I've known the Savages since they moved to our town a while back. If you think you pay a great deal in taxes, you should see their bill. And they pay on time, too. None of this dicking around with late fees either."

"I don't believe you. I pay the most, and I'll have you know that I'm never late either." She looked ready to say more, but he cut her off. Talking to his bailiff, she waited like the rest of them to see what was going on. When he turned back to her, he didn't look happy. "I can't see any reason for you to be out and about when you're obviously a threat to this child and his mother. Not that I don't think Mr. Savage can handle a woman like you, but I do want to make sure that they're safe.

Ninety days in jail with no time served. You'll behave yourself, too, while in jail, or I'll have to come back here and sentence you to a bit longer. I might well enjoy that too."

When the smack of his gavel hit the desk, everyone jumped just a little. The bailiff came back with a sheet of paper, and he'd bet anything that it was a copy of their marriage certificate. As soon as it was handed to Janice, she made a sound like a dog, growling deep in her throat like she'd been told her dinner wasn't coming to her.

"What's my bail? I have things to see to, since you're not. And don't think I'm going to be spending anymore time in jail. That's for reprobates, and I'm certainly not one of those." The judge said that he'd passed his judgment and that was all there was to be said about it. "Well, I don't care for your judgment, so take it back and give me something that I can work with. I have things that need taking care of, and I'm not getting anything done, being stuck behind bars like a criminal. Either do what I say or find me someone who will. I'm sick of messing with you."

He wouldn't budge on his decision. Shanda was able to get out on just a fine, but she had to spend the next three months behind bars like she'd done something wrong. And she hadn't. Just a little hit to her mouth shouldn't have had her spend anymore than an hour in jail. Just long enough for her to pay a fine or something. Not that she would have paid it, but now this was war. She was either going to have to hire someone to kill off the lot of them, or she was going to get nothing that she wanted. And Janice always got what she wanted.

Going back to the jail, she was plotting what needed to be done. There really wasn't that much she could do behind bars, but she could make things happen in her favor so long as she had her attorney looking out for her. He'd better, too. For as much as she was paying him, he should pull the trigger on the girl and be happy that she'd asked him to do it for her.

It took her two hours to settle down. Her head was pounding again, and she didn't much care for the fact that they'd not give her anything for it until she saw a doctor. She didn't need to see a stupid doctor. All she needed was a couple of acetaminophen, and she'd be fine. Rules were beginning to be her worst adversary, and she didn't know how much longer she was going to have to be in jail before she had to make some heads roll.

It was going to be Lisa's head that went off first. The woman was giving her fits, and she didn't like it. The very fact that she'd not even come to the courthouse where she could see her made her pissed off again. It seemed like everything was pissing her off, and she needed to get control of her temper, or she was going to have another heart attack.

Her quack of a doctor had told her that she needed to be a little less stressed all the time. He, of course, thought that she needed to go on a cruise or something that would relax her. Like she had time for that. She had a grandson to raise, and she wasn't getting any closer to doing that than she'd been before. Things were just not going in her favor, and she was going to have to see about that, too.

Lunch was brought to her, and it was another five-star meal. Not that she'd say that to anyone if asked. She'd just tell them that it had been adequate and that would be the end of it for her as far as she was concerned. Her head was still bothering her, so she laid down on her bed and wondered if her attorney had had any luck in getting her better accommodations. She really wanted her bed from home; it was perfect, but there was barely enough room in the cell for the one that she had. She didn't think that there would be enough room for her king-sized bed in the room, too.

Janice thought about her son. She'd told him not to marry Lisa. That she wouldn't be a good wife. But he had said that he loved her, and she couldn't fault him for that. She did wonder what he'd think about the mess that was going on now. He'd be rolling over in his grave if he could see how she was being treated by his wife.

She'd had him convinced that they should live with her. The house was certainly big enough, and she'd make sure that Lisa was doing a good job in raising her grandson. But things had turned out badly in that avenue, and she hurt still that she'd not insisted they move in sooner. She'd have everything that she wanted, and then some, and things would be perfect for them all.

But even after telling Lisa that David had wanted things to go her way, she'd found herself a house to live in, and that was the end of it. It had taken her three years to get the house bought so that she could control things. But she'd never been late on her rent ever, and even when she raised it twice in one year, the only thing she did was tell her that she needed thirty days' notice for that to happen. She'd been right as it turned out, and that had pissed her off too.

Then, instead of moving in with her when she raised her rent again, she'd whored herself out and moved in with that Savage person. She'd have to have his life looked into, too. There was no way that she was going to leave David to stay with a man who had bad things in his past. As soon as she got to see her attorney again, she was going to make sure he dug up something on the man and his entire family. She was leaving nothing to chance when she wanted David to live with her.

It took her most of the afternoon to get rid of her headache. Then, when her supper was brought to her, she nearly couldn't eat it as her belly was upset. Asking again for something for both, she was told that the doctor would be there in the morning to see her.

"My head hurts now. It might not hurt in the morning." He told her that was the best that he could do. "So in other words, you're doing the minimum you have to do to take care that I'm not ill. Don't think that I'm not making notes on how I'm being treated. When I own this town, I'm going to make sure that this so-called police station is torn down, and you'll be out of work. There isn't any reason for this town to have a police force when I can rule things just as easily."

When he laughed at her, she wanted to grab him by the neck and pound his head against the bars. Christ, no one understood the things she could do if she were in charge. Well, she'd show them. It was going to be her way, or there would be nothing left of this little town but herself and a couple of homes that she'd rent out. If she couldn't, then that would be just one more thing that she would deal with. People were going to do what she wanted, or there was going to be hell to pay.

Chapter 7

Lisa didn't know when it had happened, but she'd fallen in love with Brenin. His kindness was more than she could have hoped for in dealing with things, and when she realized that she'd fallen in love with him, she also realized that she wanted him to make love to her, too. It was well past time for them to be a couple, and she felt bad that she'd been making him wait for her to get on the ball.

Not sure what to do about Davy when things started to heat up, she just figured that she'd invite Brenin to her room and go from there. She'd not had sex since her husband had died, and she felt like she might be a little rusty on how things went. However, she had an idea that making love with Brenin would be something akin to the world moving beneath her feet. Waiting for him to get home, she decided that she was going to contact him through the link that they had and see what he had thought about making love with her.

"It's Lisa. I was wondering if you'd like to have sex with me." He laughed, and she could feel it all the way to her toes. It wasn't full of humor like she'd expected

from him, but it sounded lusty. She had no idea where that thought had come from. *"I've been thinking about you a lot lately, and I've fallen in love with you, too."*

"I can come home right now, and we can get started on it." She laughed with him, and she felt less nervous than she'd been before. *"I would love to make love with you. But we should wait until Davy goes to bed and is asleep. I plan on making you scream out your releases until you're unable to move."*

She wanted that too and told him so. As soon as she closed the connection, she thought of all the things that she wanted to do to him. Shivering at the thought of making love tonight, she hoped that Brenin enjoyed it as much as she hoped that she would. It was something that she didn't have a great deal of experience in, but was willing to try anything where he was concerned.

When Davy got home, he seemed to be in a good mood. He loved riding the bus and was making friends on it, older and younger than he was. But he was getting home later than he normally would if she'd picked him up. That was wearing on him, too. By the time it was bedtime for him, he was exhausted. She hoped that he'd get used to the later hour soon.

They were grilling out tonight as the weather had turned warmer. The snow from the other day had melted off quickly as the ground was still warm, but they were expecting another storm this weekend. She didn't like driving in the bad weather and hated that Brenin had to, but he promised her that he drove carefully and wasn't taking any chances. She hoped not tonight, especially. She wanted him home for the night to have sex with him.

Dinner was finished by six, and they were all in the living room. Her belly was full, and she felt sleepy too. When eight o'clock rolled around, it was Brenin who took Davy up to bed, getting him ready with his bath and all, and she couldn't have been happier. By the time he came back down at eight-thirty, she was dragging.

"Davy had me read to him tonight instead of him reading to me. I enjoyed that. He does really well for a first grader, doesn't he?" She said it was because he was in preschool for so long that he'd learned a great deal from the teachers. "I'm proud of him. He also asked if he could call me dad and had me spell out Savage for him. He said that he wasn't doing it yet, but he couldn't wait for that to be his last name. Did he say why he didn't want to be a Manchester anymore?"

"I think it has to do with his grandma. She's been telling him that he was going to have to find himself a good wife—and that she'd help him pick her out and carry on the Manchester name. He is also supposed to name his son David Eugene, like his father had been.

To be honest with you, I never thought that David liked his name all that much and was reluctant to call Davy that when he was born. I think his mother pressured him into that." Brenin pointed out to her that he didn't even like girls. "I know. So you can tell how that went over. Plus, she's going to help him find a good wife. I suppose that's a dig at me. I was never considered a good wife to her. It's the only time that I knew David to stand up to her when we wanted to get married."

"Pardon me, but he sounds like he needed a swift kick to the ass. She mentioned once how she'd convinced him that you all were going to live with her. Did he ever talk to you about that?" She told Brenin that it would never have happened. She'd told him right off that she would have left him had he mentioned it again. "I guess her version is that she convinced him, no matter what he said to her. That sounds like something that she'd do. Make things out to be all one-sided since he wasn't here to dispute her word."

"I can see that as well." She busied herself with the papers that she'd been grading as he read his book. She loved that he liked to read, and some of it she hoped would rub off on Davy. Even though he'd read his five pages a night, he didn't much care for reading on his own. That was why she was glad that Brenin was reading his book to her boy, as he might find it interesting.

At nine o'clock, she was ready to call it a day. Telling Brenin that she was going to bed, he said he'd be up in a minute or two as he was going to make sure that the house was locked up tight. By the time she'd showered and gotten ready for bed, her body was on pins and needles. As soon as she heard the doorknob turn, she became anxious about what was to happen. At least she hoped would happen.

"I was afraid that I'd gone to the wrong bedroom. When you said you wanted to make love, I had hoped that you'd want me in this room." She blurted out that she'd take him in any room and covered her mouth with her hand. "Nervous? You have no reason to be. It'll happen or it won't. I'm not going to rush you into anything that you don't want."

"I know that too. I am nervous." She made her way to the bed, and he stopped her. "You've changed your mind?"

"No. I want to undress you. I want to see what delights you have hidden under your gown." He moved toward her, and it was almost as if he was gliding. When he was close enough to touch, she buried her nose in his neck and inhaled deeply. She'd been wanting to do that for weeks now and hadn't been willing to try it. "You're making it hard for me to go slow with you. I planned on making this last for a while."

"I want you now." Putting her hand on his chest, she could feel his heart beating. "Mine is beating so fast, I bet you can hear it."

"I can. I can smell you too. You smell like the earth and sun all wrapped up in one lovely piece of a woman." When he pulled her toward him, she followed. Lifting her chin up, he kissed her gently on the mouth. Moaning, she wanted more of him. But he was taking his time with her. As soon as she was flush with his body, she could feel his cock and squirmed a little, getting closer to him. "You're making me crazy with need, love. Don't you want this to last?"

"Next time." She reached between them and began opening up his shirt. His tie had been taken off when he'd gotten home from work, and she was glad. She wasn't sure how to remove that and didn't want to look foolish. "You have way too many clothes on. I want you naked so that I can look at you too."

Getting his shirt off, she worked on the belt he had on. He really did have too many clothes on, and she was getting frustrated with him because he was just standing there. Finally looking up at him, she couldn't believe that he was smiling. Asking him what he found so funny, she finally just jerked the belt free of the loops and tossed it across the room.

"You're funny." She thought that he was making fun of her and took a step back from him. "No, don't stop. Please. If you have trouble with something, just tear it from my body. I'm enjoying you undressing me."

Finally, to the point where she could get his pants undone, all she did was unbutton the top snap and pull his zipper down enough that she could touch him. Sliding her hand into his pants, wrapping her hand around his thick cock, she sighed heavily. This was what she wanted.

"I've thought of this for several days now. How I would undress you or you me. It's not turning out like I thought it would, but now that I can hold you, I feel like it was well worth it. You're so very thick, aren't you?" He nodded, kissing her on the neck and shoulder. "I love that. It feels like you're trying to find a place to bite me. I think that I'd like that too."

"I'm going to bite you when you come with me. I want to taste your hot spicy blood while you're coming." He nipped at her skin, and she felt herself get wetter. "I bet if I touched you right now, you'd come for me. I want to taste your pussy, love. I want to drink from you until you are ripe for me."

Guiding her to the bed, he sat her on the side of it. Whatever he wanted to do, she was willing. Right now her body ached to come and be with him, but she knew too that when he ate her, she was going to enjoy it more than anything that she'd ever done with sex before. Having her remove her panties, she felt her first bit of embarrassment. He seemed to understand and spread her legs apart for what he wanted to do.

As he lowered his head to her heat, she inhaled deeply and waited for him to touch her. As soon as he suckled on her clit, she came apart, screaming out his name. After that, it was her coming so much that she was dizzy with it. But he never stopped, no matter how much she begged him to.

Finally, when she got him to stop his relentless eating her, she begged him to take her. It was that, or she was going to have to do something for herself. While he did seem to think on that, she wanted his cock inside of her now. Instead of waiting for him to decide, she pulled him in for a kiss that had her tasting bits of herself on his mouth. It was erotic and exciting at the same time.

Moving around on the bed so that she was in the middle of it, he crawled up her body, touching her as he went. Sometimes he would nip at her flesh, suckle at her breast, lick along her ribs, but he never stopped touching her. When he took her hands to the top of the bed and held them there, his other hand ran up and down her ribs. Making her skin feel like silk. When his cock was at her entrance, she shivered slightly. Looking up at him, he told her that he loved her as he slowly slid into her.

Nothing could have prepared her for the way it felt to have him inside of her. It was as if they were one person; her pussy to his cock made her feel things that she'd never felt before. Loved for sure, but also cherished. Wrapping her arms around his shoulders when he released her, she held onto him as he slowly fucked her.

He made love to her mouth, her hands. As he was fucking her faster, his cock doing things to her that she loved, he tasted her mouth with his own. As soon as he told her that he was coming, her body separated and came back together gently, like a nice summer storm that brought her over the edge with him. As they both laid there panting, she knew that she would love him for the rest of her days. He was the best thing that had ever happened to her.

Waking up, she wondered what was going on for a few seconds when she heard breathing beside her. Brenin was there, his body curled around her own like it was meant to be. As she rolled to her side, thinking of getting up so that she could go to the bathroom, he pulled her in tighter and held her to him. Finally, after telling him she needed to get up, he rolled to his side and let her go. Getting up quickly, the floor was cold, she made her way to the bathroom, and while washing her hands, she smiled at the reflection in the mirror.

"You're sappy." Giggling lightly, she made her

way to the bed again and got in with Brenin. He was still warm, but for his feet, and she nearly cried out when he touched them to her own. As soon as they were warmed up, she fell back to sleep and didn't stir at all. This was the way to sleep with a person, with love and compassion.

She felt energized when she got up. While she knew that some more magic was going to come to her, she didn't feel any ill effects as she heard that she would. Maybe she'd had enough was all she could think about, and she was fine with that too.

As soon as she was in her makeshift office in the dining room, she began working on the papers that she needed to grade. Since Brenin's side of the bed was empty when she got up, the only thing that she could think of was that he'd gotten up to go to work after taking Davy to the bus stop at the end of their driveway.

She missed seeing Davy in the morning and decided that she wasn't going to make a habit of sleeping so late. It started off her day in the right direction when she got a hug from her little man and missed him throughout the morning. When she heard from Brenin about dinner plans tonight, she was excited to be able to have dinner with Tucker and Kaida. They were the best couple that she'd had as role models, and she loved how they seemed to not be able to get enough of each other. They were adorable together.

~*~

Tucker liked Lisa. She was funny and easy to talk to. She seemed to have a good head on her shoulders as well. He knew that the two of them had bonded, and he wanted to ask her about that. But he was afraid that it would come off wrong when all he wanted to know was if it had hurt her like it had the other women in the family. He thought Lady Earth had it right in saying that after something so beautiful as bonding, there was no point in making it so painful to get the magic. He also noticed that they couldn't stop touching one another either. A good sign, as far as he was concerned, that things were finally going well between them.

"I couldn't help but realize that the two of you haven't been married all that long. To see you two together, it looks like you've been together for decades instead of only a few weeks. That's the way I see it anyway." Tucker told Lisa that he felt that way, too, like he'd been waiting for his little dragon for all his life. "I'm told that Kaida means little dragon. Is that what you plan on calling her for the rest of your lives together?"

"It is. I love that she's my little dragon, and I was lucky in that she never took me to task all that much when we first met. I wasn't what anyone would call romantic." Kaida laughed and said he'd gotten that right. "I'm sorry to say that I wasn't even a nice person simply because she was human. I'd written them all off as monsters until meeting her, and didn't want to have anything to do with any of them. But she wore me down and made me see her for what she is. A beautiful dragon that holds every part of my heart in her hand."

"I might have thought that was sappy a few weeks ago. Even a couple of days ago, but since I feel the same way about Brenin, I can relate to what you're saying. It's wonderful having someone that you can love unconditionally, isn't it?" Tucker and Kaida agreed with her, and she sat up higher in her seat. "I love you guys, too. Meeting all of you has been like a dream come true for me. Having great friends is something that I've never had before now. It's a heady feeling having people in your corner that you can depend on all the time."

They talked about the weather too while waiting for dinner to be called. Even Davy joined in on the conversation at times, and she was proud of him for being so polite and a good boy. It was Kaida who asked about Mrs. Manchester, and she told her that she was in jail for now but didn't know how much longer.

"I'm sorry, I thought that I told you. She's going to be in jail for the next three months. At least that long, I'm happy to say." She asked Brenin what charges she was being held on. "Mostly it's to do with her wanting to kill you. She did threaten the judge, too, but I'm not sure he put that in her requirement for being in jail. Janice wants you under her control, and if you don't do what you're supposed to do, then she's going to kill you and take Davy anyway. I'm glad that you're immortal. There is no telling what she'd do if you were to be anywhere around her if not. She wants to control you and have Davy raised the way that she feels good about. I'm assuming that she's talking about how she raised David, her son."

"He didn't much care for his mom. I was surprised when he told me that she wanted us all to live with her and he was considering it. I told him that it wasn't going to happen, and he was all right with that. However, I think she was wearing him down. I swear that she could beat a poor horse to death when she got something in her head. It's like she has a one-track mind where things are to go her way or she's going to kill someone." Lisa shivered slightly and told them all that she made her nervous. "If she gets out anytime soon, she's going to make my life a living hell until she does something stupid. I hope that it doesn't come to that, but with her it's hard to know what she'll do."

"She'll do something stupid and end up on the wrong side of our dragons. We are all here to protect you, love." She nodded to Tucker and thanked him. "No need for that. We're all family right now, and we protect what's ours. You and Davy have come to mean a great deal to us all, too."

"Thank you again. The two of us have had a wonderful life with you all in it and I think I can say this for us both when I say I've never had such good friends before." Tucker nodded and his cheeks turned a bright red. She loved it when he was embarrassed and never gave up the opportunity to do so to him. For a man as old as he was, he certainly embarrassed easily. Davy said he had one friend that was better and that was his friend Toby. "I talked to his mother the other day. She said that she wants us to wait before bringing Davy into see her son. He's been beaten up badly."

"I have some news on Tommy Benson. He's the bully who has beaten up other kids at the school. He's been sent to military school for the duration. I don't think his parents were given a choice in whether or not he went. It was there or jail." She asked what they were going to do about the hospital bill for young Toby. "They're picking up the tab on it and anything else he has to have done while recuperating, too. I've heard that he's going to need more surgeries to put his face back together." Davy started crying then, and Tucker said he was sorry.

"He took the beating for me. He told me that I was littler than him, so he could take it. It might have killed me had it been me, and I'm so happy that he's my friend." Brenin held onto Davy while he cried. "I wish I could see him again. He's my bestest friend in the world, and I hate that he got hurt like he did."

"As soon as his mom says it's all right, we'll go and see him. She will be the one who decides if he's well enough to have visitors. It's really important that we keep him in our thoughts for now and make sure that we keep away until he's better enough to enjoy our company. Right now, they have to be afraid of germs, too. You don't want to take him something like a cold right now. We want him to get better, don't we?" Davy said that he missed him. "I tell you what. Tomorrow we'll go and get him a card that you can send to him. And some flowers for his mom. She must be missing everyone, too, with her being in the hospital all the time with her only child."

"I'd like that very much." After they were called to dinner, Davy said that he was starving. He'd not had any after-school snack tonight as they headed right over to Tucker's home for dinner. She was going to have to be more careful of that in the future. She didn't want him to starve when it came to eating his meals, she thought with a smile. "Mr. Tucker, is it all right to call you Uncle Tucker? You're going to be my uncle for sure once I get adopted. I'll be Davy Eugene Savage. Doesn't that sound good?"

"It does, buddy. It really does." Tucker messed with his hair and hugged him. "You should call us all your uncles and the ladies' aunt. I'm sure they'd enjoy that very much. I know that I would."

"Good. Then I'll call them all uncle. Brenin said that I could call him dad when I'm ready. I never knew my real dad, but for what grandma tells me." Davy looked like he was thinking on things before he spoke again. "I don't think he was as perfect as she said that he is. Mom tells me nobody is perfect, but she said that he was. I'm not going to stay with her anymore until she gets better. Mom said that she wants to hurt her so that I have to live with her. I don't want to do that. I don't much like her anyway."

Brenin helped her son cut up his burger and fries so he could pick them up. It was a big burger, but she'd bet that he'd have no trouble eating it all. And it was perfect, just the way that he liked it, with just catsup on it and nothing else. When he ate the first half, she knew that he was going to finish it all. He was going through a growth spurt and would eat just about anything that was put in front of him.

After dinner, they went to the living room. There was a preseason football game on, and they sat around watching it. While she nor Davy knew that much about football, they enjoyed watching the others enjoying it. They were loud about some of the calls, but they laughed, too. While living with Brenin, she knew that she was going to have to learn more about the sport that they all seemed to appreciate watching.

Going home that night, Brenin had to carry Davy into the house. He'd always been a heavy sleeper, and she was glad that someone could carry him still. She couldn't do it and would end up getting him awake enough to walk inside. He was seven and heavy for her to try to manage on her own.

Once he was in bed and tucked in, she left him to his sleep and went to find Brenin. He was in the office on his computer, looking at some of the stocks that Tucker had told him about.

Apparently, Trevor, son to Kings and Skye, knew a little bit of magic that would allow him to see the futures on some investments, and he wanted to get right on them. Even though she'd heard that the Savage family had all the money, it made her feel good that he still invested when he wanted to have more money coming in all the time.

She didn't believe for a moment that they had all the money, but she knew that they had quite a bit of it. How much? She wasn't sure, but she was willing to bet that it was several billion dollars. If it was more than that, she didn't want to know. The amount that she had in her head was more than enough zeros for her to think about.

Going up to bed at ten-thirty, she was in bed with the lights off by eleven. Her body was still sore from making love last night. She hoped that Brenin would make love to her again tonight and every night for the rest of their lives together. She loved the way that he was tender to her and loved her so much.

When he came up to bed a little after eleven, she was ready for him. As soon as he got into bed with her, he made the same kind of love he'd done with her last night. Her body responded to his like it was made for him, and she loved it. After coming several times, she was pleasantly exhausted and ready for sleep. Brenin held her throughout the night.

The bed was empty again when she woke. She was getting really bad at sleeping late and thought about setting an alarm so that she'd be up with the men in her life. Missing Davy before he got off to school was something that she didn't care for and set her alarm on her phone so that she'd get up in the morning. He wasn't going to be seven forever, and she didn't want to miss a moment of his life.

Brenin was having breakfast when she got to the kitchen. He told her that they were running behind this morning, and Davy was going to eat at school. The program was a good one where kids could eat their first meal of the day at the school, and she didn't mind him doing it. Once in a while. She thought that he ate better at home and thought that was another reason for her to be getting up with them. She could make him something to eat if the cook was running behind, too.

"He needed something signed about a permission slip for a trip they're taking to the art museum in Zanesville. Since you had it marked on the calendar, I went ahead and signed it." She said that was fine; his name was on the paperwork to sign off on things like that. "I also heard from Ace. My adoption paperwork is on the judge's desk as we speak, so that we can get the adoption paperwork finished up. It might be sooner than we think that he'll be another Savage."

"That's what he wants more than anything. To no longer be a Manchester when everyone around him is a Savage." He asked her how Janice might react. "I don't know. I'm not going to tell her until I have to, and I see no reason why she needs to know now. We'll just keep that between all of us."

"I hoped that you'd say that. She'll find out someday, but we don't have to rub it in her face for now." She agreed with Brenin. "I love you, Lisa Savage. It's going to be nice to have Davy Savage in our family too, don't you think?"

"I think he's going to love it. He's already asking

me how to spell it. As you can imagine, that word doesn't come up on his site words all that often." The two of them laughed and got up from the breakfast table. They both had things to do, and she wanted to get a good start on her paperwork. So far, she was doing well with grading papers and thought that she could do it for a while yet. She was glad too that it didn't take away from her Davy and Brenin time, too.

Chapter 8

Stretching out on the bed, Brenin decided that he needed a nap for just a bit longer. He'd been sleeping well when he finally got to sleep, but he was making love to Lisa both at night and in the morning. He couldn't believe that she seemed so energized in the morning when he was just dragging his butt.

He must be doing something wrong, was all he could figure out, or she was just in better shape than he was. Even his dragon seemed to be lazing about when they were around town. Getting up, he took a long, hot shower and got dressed, thankful for the magic that allowed him to dress as he wanted, or he'd be more tired.

Getting breakfast, Lisa was already hard at work on her paperwork. He ate his first meal of the day and dragged his butt to work. She asked him if he was all right, and all he could manage was a grunt to her. His entire body felt like it needed to be covered up with a heavy blanket and left alone to die. When he got to work, he didn't even bother turning on his computer, but leaned his head back on his chair and closed his eyes. It was that or get nothing done, but looking at the screen without seeing anything.

Waking up once when his phone gave a short ring, he had not even bothered to turn the service over for him to pick up. Deciding that he was going to leave the service on for a while longer, he leaned back again and closed his eyes. He couldn't believe how exhausted he was and thought that it had nothing to do with all the sex they were having. He just wouldn't believe that a human woman could outdo him.

It was almost noon when he opened his eyes. He didn't feel any better, but he had to go to the bathroom. As soon as he started to pee, he knew something was wrong with him. His urine was a bright rust color, and he was worried. Reaching out to Kings, the only one he knew that might know, he told him what was going on and how he was feeling. Then he told him about his urine being so bright. Like it was iron colored.

"I'm coming to you. I've read about something like this. It's iron in your system. How's your dragon feeling?" He said that he didn't even know if he could shift right now; the two of them were so exhausted. "That's not good either. I'll be there in about ten minutes. I'm going to have Skye look something up for us in the books we have here. I'm also going to send Lady Earth to you. This sounds serious."

The queen was in his office when he staggered his way there. He wanted Lisa there, too, but also didn't want to worry her. If there was iron in his system, then it could mean death to both him and his dragon. Changing his mind, he asked Kings to pick up Lisa on the way, thinking that if he was dying, he wanted things to be said to his mate.

"It's not just you that's sick. It's Ace too. He's been done for the past two days." Kings asked him to take off his shirt, and he did so. "See the markings here. Those red circles are the iron deposits in your bloodstream. We have to figure out a way to get it out of you."

"I'm going to be sick." He puked up all his breakfast and felt a little better. As soon as he held onto Lisa's hand, he felt a little better, but he was going to die if they didn't figure this out, and he didn't want to. He'd just found his mate, and he was in love with her. What was Davy going to say when he couldn't be a Savage because he'd died? "I don't want to die."

"I don't want you to die either." Lisa was crying as he held her. "Where did the iron come from? It's not me. I read about iron in the body in one of those books that Skye gave me. Why didn't you say something sooner?"

"I thought it was just me. That I couldn't keep up with you." She smacked him on the arm, and he smiled. "Well, that's the only thing that's been different in my life. I've been having copious amounts of sex with you. How bad is Ace? Did you know that we have a cup of tea every morning? I wondered why he'd not been around for the last couple of days. He must really be ill." He felt himself fading again and held onto Lisa as tightly as he could. She was all he had in the world, and he was going to fade away with his dragon. Asking Lady Earth what he was to do now, she said that she was going to drain the iron from him and that should do the trick. At some point, he must have passed out because he woke once to see Lisa sobbing in the corner of the room.

"You're dying, buddy. I had no idea that iron could do that to someone so quickly. Ace is about there, too. Lady Earth is doing all she can for the two of you, but it's draining her as well." He asked Kings to save Ace, as he was the mayor. "We're going to save you both if we can. Now be quiet so that she can work on you."

The world just faded away. All the colors first, then the items around the room. Reaching for Lisa, he held tightly to her hand and told her how much he loved her. It was getting more difficult to breathe, and he could hear his heart beginning to slow. Telling Lisa that he loved her once again, he felt himself just slipping away.

He woke once to so much pain that he nearly let go of his dragon. The pain for them both was nearly unbearable, and he wasn't coping with it at all. When the world went dark again, it was all he could do not to sob like a small child; he hurt so badly.

Ace was lying next to him when he woke again. He knew that he was at his end when he couldn't even lift his arm to hold onto Lisa. Nothing in his body was working, and it wasn't until the Lady Earth put her hands on his chest that the unbearable pain came back. It was like he was in a nightmare of pain when she did that, and he didn't have the strength to stop her from doing whatever she was doing. When he passed out this time, he wondered how much longer he was going to suffer before he was simply gone. Right now, the only thing holding him to this earth was the fact that he got to see Lisa when he opened his eyes. And that was well worth all the pain that he was enduring right now. He could no longer hold her in his arms, but he knew that she was close. He could smell her and her fear. It hurt his heart when he realized that he'd never be able to see his child born, and he was so happy for the chance to see Davy as his son.

Brenin couldn't count the times that he was awakened by pain. Every time he woke up, he'd be so weak that he couldn't cry out anymore. Lady Earth was trying her best, but he knew that at some point she was going to rest, and that would be soon. She was fading too, and he didn't have the strength to tell her to stop what she was doing before it was too late for her as well. He never saw Ace again, moving his head was too difficult. But he knew that he was close. He hoped that he lived on. The man had done wonders for the little town that they lived in.

It was dark when he opened his eyes this time. He didn't move, not that he could, but he just looked around with his eyes. He didn't smell anyone in the room, but didn't know if that ability had left him as well. He couldn't even smell Lisa in the room with him and knew that she'd never leave him.

"You gave us quite a scare, Lord Brenin." It was his faerie, but for the life of him, he couldn't remember his name. "Cup, sir. I'm Cup Cake. You call me Cup." He nodded and was nearly sick again. "Just lie there and be quiet, sir. You're on the mend now, and you should be resting to get stronger."

"Lisa?" He was told she was beside him as she wouldn't leave him. "Hurt. So much." Cup seemed to understand and put her fingers to his forehead. He felt himself fading into sleep, but not like before. He was going to rest now, and he was getting better. He hoped so. He still didn't want to die.

He woke up over the next few times he'd been resting. He didn't know if it was days or hours, he just knew that he was feeling stronger. Once, he asked about Ace and was told that he was still out and would be for a while yet. Whatever that meant, they didn't tell him that he was still dying, and he felt like he could rest better than before. As soon as Lisa touched him with her hands, he curled them up around his chest and held her. He was getting stronger but not out of the woods, yet he was told.

Kings was near the bed when he woke up again. He smiled at him, and he smiled back. He took his hand into his and told him that Lisa had been made to go to her room to rest, as she was going to be sick if she didn't.

"She didn't want to, as you can well imagine, but I told her she was going to do you no good if she was down too when you needed her. Also, the faeries gave her a little bit of magic to make sure that she could rest well. I'll say this again, they're good to have around." He asked about Ace. "He had more of the iron in his system than you did."

"Did you figure out who was giving it to us?" He told him what they'd been able to find out. "So it was in the tea we were drinking. Tank didn't like the taste, so it was all Ace and I could have of it."

"It was for iron-poor blood. You guys were drinking it daily, and that was why it had been hard on your bodies. Since you were ingesting it slowly over time, it took a while for it to show up. If not for you mentioning the tea that you two drank in the morning together, we might not have been able to figure it out. The only thing that I have to say is read the labels from now on. It might well save your life."

"I will. Christ, I've never felt like this before." He said he'd appreciate it if he never felt that way again. "I promise you I'm going to be more careful about what I ingest from now on."

"Good." He must have fallen asleep again because when he woke up, Lisa was sitting in the chair that Kings had been in.

Taking her hand into his, he watched her as she slept. It was good to be able to see her again after all he'd been through, and he was glad that she was resting. He was going to need her to be healthy when he was up and around. He had a feeling that he was going to be weak for a while yet and was going to depend on her to be there for him.

"You look better." He nodded and told her that he was feeling bad still, but was feeling better now. "I missed you. Kings made me take a nap. I'm glad that I did. I feel better, too. And just seeing you looking better makes me feel good too."

"I was terrified that I was going to die. I had no idea that iron could do that to us." She told him it was something else to blame on his parents. "I believe you're right. Half of my lack of knowledge is because of them. I'm going to read those books that Kings has. I know that they'll be helpful in all kinds of things. Who knew that a cup of tea in the morning with a good friend could cause so much damage to myself."

"I'm going to start reading labels, too, from now on. I want to make sure that we're both around for a good long time." He asked her how long he'd been out. "Ten days. Mostly, you were sleeping, but once you started to get better, you weren't out all that long. It was terrible seeing you suffer the way that you were. I love you, Brenin."

"And I love you. I'm so glad that you were by my side all this time. It gave me something to look forward to when I woke up. Just seeing you now is something that I worried that I'd never see again." Lisa leaned down and kissed him. "I love you so much, my heart. I don't know what I'd do without you in my life. You saved my life just by being here with me all the time."

"I don't want you to be sick like that again, deal? I don't want to live my life without you in it." She kissed him again. "Davy is worried about you, too. When I told him that you were getting better, he burst into tears and said he was going to call you Dad from now on. He said that he loved you as well."

"I love him too. Like he was my own son. I'd be honored to be called dad by him, and I'd think of him as my son forever." She wiped at the tears on her cheeks, and he told her he was sorry that he'd upset her. "I promise that I'm going to take better care of myself from now on. You'll be sick of me being around. I'm going to show you how much I love you daily. No, hourly. You make me want to be a better man."

Tired again, he closed his eyes. Something that Kings had told him was that he was to rest when he needed to. That the poison was all gone, but it had effects on his body that they didn't know about yet. Taking him at his word, he smiled a little as he let sleep take him under.

~*~

Lisa could rest better now, and she even was able to take a nap during the day to combat the exhaustion that she'd felt while Brenin was down. It had been two weeks since he woke up and was talking, but she could see improvements every day.

Tonight, he and the others were going to shift into their dragons and fly in the sky. She wasn't joining them this time as she was still having trouble with lift off. While she loved being a dragon, there were so many things that she had to remember so she'd not hurt anyone, while the other part of her. Like her tail.

She'd nearly taken out the new pool house when she'd been swinging it around. After that, she curled it up under her body and made sure that it didn't get away from her again. As it was now, the pool house was going to have the roof repaired and one of the walls replaced. It was a good thing that she was smaller than the other dragons, or she might well have taken out the pool too.

Laughing to herself, she finished the stack of papers that she'd been grading and made notes on the ones that had been exactly alike. Word-for-word, the two papers were identical, and she was sure that they cheated. All the answers were right, too. She didn't grade them, thinking that the teacher would need to go over them with the students, and started on her next stack of papers. She'd gotten into grading a second-grade class for paperwork and was loving the answers that the kids gave. Some of them were so funny.

She was just finishing up her work when it was time to go and get Davy at the end of the drive. Thanks to Lady Earth they had a troll at the end of their drive to make sure people couldn't just come around when they wanted. He looked like a human to any other humans that came around, but to shifters, he was the biggest troll that she'd ever seen. Of course, he was her first one, but she thought that he was bigger than most.

Driving to the end of the drive, it had turned cold again, and she was ready for him to get off the bus when it stopped in front of the drive. When Davy got off and waved at Gruff, the troll, she wondered how he was so calm around the big guy. She knew that he saw a troll when he looked at the man, but he made her nervous. Not that he'd hurt either one of them, but he was just so large. Turning around in the driveway, she made her way back up to the house for snack time.

"I have to read ten pages now." She asked him if the teacher knew he usually read more than that anyway. "I told her, and she said that was good. That it would be no problem for me to read fifteen. I love to read, and so does Dad."

"He does. I know that he enjoys reading to you at night, too." He nodded, and they went over his sight words twice before he got them all right. "We'll get you a new stack added to this one soon. I'm betting that the teacher will be happy with your progress when grade cards come out."

"She told me that I'm smart, but I don't make fun of the kids who are struggling. Sometimes she asks me to go over the words with some of the classmates so that I can help them learn. It helps me too." Lisa said she was proud of him. "I'm proud of myself, too. I love helping the other kids with their homework."

He was starting to add numbers now, and she couldn't believe they were advancing so much in first grade. He could do it; Davy had been adding items up for a long time. He could subtract, too, which she thought was good. When she gave him his snack of carrots and dressing, he plowed through them like he'd been starved. She knew that he ate earlier in the day and probably was starving when he got home. Davy could burn a lot of energy when he was playing on the playground, too.

After he finished with his homework and put it all away, she handed him an ice cream bar because she was so proud of him. Eating it at the table, she wondered how she'd been so lucky to have had him in her life. And now that she had Brenin too, she was someone who couldn't contain her happiness.

"I was thinking about something. This is going to be our first Christmas in this house. Do you think it's going to be all right with Santa Claus that we don't live in the other house anymore?" She'd forgotten that he still believed in Santa and told him he'd have no trouble finding him. "I'm going to write him a letter and let him know that we've moved anyway. I don't want him to go there and find an empty house."

"All right. When you want to do that, we'll take care of it." He said he was thinking about getting his dad to help him. "Whatever you want. I'm sure that he'll be happy to help you with your letter."

She was a little bit hurt that he wanted Brenin to help with his letter. But she was learning to share duties with him so that he and Davy could be closer. She knew that she couldn't be selfish with things like this, but it still hurt her just enough that she had to fight tears.

Getting the mess cleaned up that he'd made, the cook said they were going to have roast beef for dinner and that Lord Brenin had approved the pie that she'd made. She was sure that he had. Brenin loved pie more than he did any other food. And if it was still warm with ice cream on it, he was even more happy.

She and Davy watched some television before Brenin got home. It was some show that she kind of liked about a family of dogs. It taught some good lessons, and she was glad that she didn't watch too much of it. The dogs and their antics got on her nerves a bit. Laughing at herself, she knew she wasn't their target audience.

"It's snowing again." She looked out the window and saw that it was indeed snowing. It was coming down in big flakes that looked like they were as big as quarters. "I hope that Dad drives carefully. He just got his new car, and I like it. Yours is great too. I love that we don't have to worry about getting stuck in the driveway."

"They usually have it plowed before we have to get out on it." She also reminded him that since it had been warm the last few days, it might not stick so much. "I hope that's the case. I'd hate for you to miss any more school due to the weather. You don't have to make up any days yet, but if the weather turns again, you might not get a spring break."

She had plans for Spring Break this year. Every year, she and Davy would fly to Florida and go to the park there. It was a nice, fun place to be, and they usually took a hotel room so that he could have breakfast with some of the characters. This year, Brenin was going to go with them, and she knew that they'd have even more fun than before. He was already making plans to be off the week, and so was she. Davy more than likely knew what they were doing and would be disappointed if they couldn't go. But she'd make it up to him with something else they could do while he was off, even if it wasn't for the entire week.

When Brenin got home, safe and sound, they sat in the living room to warm up with him. He said that the weather was supposed to turn bad overnight and not to expect school in the morning. She knew that was a possibility and was getting worried about their vacation.

She could take him out of school that week and might well do that. But she didn't want to if she didn't have to. Davy would think it was a blast to miss a little bit of school, and she didn't blame him. He loved school, but loved being able to spend time in Florida, too.

After dinner, Davy and Brenin worked on the letter to Santa. It didn't have what he wanted in it for

Christmas. She usually got him what he wanted when she could afford it, but this letter was so that he could find them. She loved how his mind worked and was happy to see the two of them with their heads together doing it.

Getting Davy ready for bed, he seemed to have all kinds of energy now that he was used to getting up earlier to catch the bus. He also got home later in the evening, too, and that was throwing off his schedule. Now that he was used to both, she could see him getting back to his old self and having a good time.

It took her a bit longer to get him settled down, but she didn't mind. He was in a good mood now, and she loved having fun with him. As he was sitting at his desk in his room when she was getting ready to leave, he told her that he loved her.

"I love you very much, too. What's going on?" He shrugged, and she went back into his room to find out what had made him seem so sad all of a sudden. "Is something going on at school that you need to talk about?"

"No. The teacher took Toby's stuff out of his desk today. It hurt my heart. She said that he'd not be back this school term and that we needed to move on. I don't want to move on without him." Davy burst into tears, and she held him. "He's going to be a grade behind me now, and we'll never have class together again. Why did that Tommy person have to hurt him? It's not fair."

"No, it's not, and he might not be behind you, honey. His mom will work with him when he's better, and he'll be able to catch up." The teacher apparently told them that he'd be in first grade again next year. "She shouldn't have said that to you guys. I know you were looking forward to having him in your class again. I'm sorry that she hurt your feelings."

"I want him to be better. Tommy is better because he beat up my friend. I want him to be better so I can have him over to the house for a pool party, too." She said that they could still do that. When he was better. "I hope he gets better soon. I really want to go and see him."

"I'll call his mom again tomorrow. I've been meaning to go and see her anyway. Maybe I need to just go and see how he's doing in person." He asked if she'd really do that. "I will. Not tomorrow, but the next day if the weather is better. I'll go and talk to her about things that she might not know. I'll tell Toby too, that you're worried about him."

"Tell him that I love him too. I want him to know that we're still best friends." She said she'd tell him that for him. "Thanks, Mom. You're the best there is."

After getting him settled in his room so that he

could relax enough to be asleep by nine, she read him more of the book they'd been reading. It was the second book in a series, and she was enjoying it as much as he was and would sometimes read a bit of it during the day when she had time.

Going up to bed later that night, she was happy to have Brenin waiting for her when she got to their room. He told her that he was feeling better all the time and wanted to make love to her again. She was actually nervous about that. Seeing how close he'd been to death had scared her to no end. She didn't want him to be that exhausted again.

Putting him off in favor of being tired herself, she went to bed and snuggled up with him. His body was stronger than it had been before, and she was glad for that. Sometimes when she closed her eyes, she could still see him, pale as a ghost and thinner than she'd ever remembered him being. His breathing had been slower too, and hearing his heart beating so slowly had her thinking again that he was going to die. Pulling him closer to her, she held him tightly, telling him how much she loved him.

"I'm all right." She said she knew that in her head but not in her heart. "I'm sorry I got sick. I never dreamed nor knew that I could get sick from having a cup of tea every morning. I'm more careful now with everything that I drink and eat. I might do that for the rest of my life."

"I'm glad to hear that." As she closed her eyes, willing herself to sleep, she remembered that she'd forgotten to set her alarm again. It was a habit that she was getting into, sleeping late, and she needed to get over that. She missed the boys in her family too much to let herself lounge in bed for half the morning.

Chapter 9

Turning off the alarm, he saw the notice from school that the school was going to be closed for the day. Thinking that he'd just rest a bit longer, he pulled the covers up and over himself and Lisa and closed his eyes. There was no point in getting up early when the buses wouldn't be running.

"I forgot to set my alarm again." He told her there was no school. "He's going to hate that. We were just talking about Spring Break last night. He's counting the days until he can take off."

"I'm looking forward to it as well. I told my cousins about it, and they're jealous." She told him that was good. "Is Trevor allowed to go with us? I knew you were going to ask Kings and Skye if he could go too."

"She said that it was totally up to him, but she didn't have a problem with him going with us. I hope he can go. It'll be fun for Davy to have someone about his age to hang out with." He said he'd bet he'd go just to be doing something on Spring Break. "I heard that he was doing something with the wolf pack, but they take the time off during that time so that they can hang out with family too." She looked up at him.

"I love you." He kissed her gently on the mouth and decided that he was going to push her just a little so she'd know he was ready to go back to making love every day. He hated to work this way, but he wanted her badly, and he knew she was still thinking that he was going to die. Deepening the kiss, he rolled her to her back and touched his hand to her breast. "I want you."

"You do?" She seemed to be surprised by that when he looked down at her with a smile. "I want you, too, but I've been worried about you being too tired."

"I'm not too tired. In fact, I think that if we made love right now, I'd be better than I have been in some time. I've had life slap me around a bit, and I want to take advantage of having a good life for the rest of my days."

He pulled her pajama shirt off and dropped it to the floor. Taking her breast into his mouth, he bit down on her nipple hard enough to have her crying out. As he worked at getting her pajama pants off, he took advantage of her distraction a bit to claim her throat. He could taste her arousal and feel her heart pounding even as he nipped at the warm flesh there.

As soon as she was naked beneath him, he rolled to his side to remove his boxers. His cock was painfully hard, and he knew that he wasn't going to be gentle with her as he'd been before. Sliding his cock deep inside of her, he moved her legs so that they were up and over his hips. He was so deep inside of her that he could feel her sheath as it milked him. Sliding in and out of her harder, he was thrilled when she asked him for more.

Pounding her faster, he took her breasts into his hands and pushed them together. Sucking and nipping at them one at a time, he nearly came when she pulled him closer to her. As her hips came up to meet his downward stroke, he knew that he wasn't going to last that much longer and worked his hand beneath her to her ass. Holding her to him, pounding her hard, he was rewarded with her biting at his neck when she came apart.

Brenin didn't join her yet; he was hoping for one more ride. As he took her to her peak again, he licked a path from her earlobe to her shoulder and bit down on her there. Coming apart with her this time, he was shocked when he came a second, then a third time. He'd not done that ever and dropped atop of Lisa when he felt like his body simply gave out.

"Are you all right?" He said he was still taking inventory. "I get that. You bit me, and it felt fantastic. Like you were marking me as your own."

"I was. So was my dragon. We needed to claim you." She giggled, and he lifted his head up just enough to look at her. "What's so funny? I just had the best sex of my life, and you're laughing at me."

"I'm laughing because you wanted to claim me. I've never been claimed before." She rolled with him to his side and then to his back. "This could be interesting."

She rode his cock as he held onto her hips. He couldn't believe that he was still hard after coming as much as he did, but was happy to be with her. As she played with her breasts, he sat up more so that he could enjoy them as well. There was something so erotic about making love first thing in the morning that had him thinking that he should have done this sooner. But she might not have wanted him just yet. The little bit of push he'd given her had been in perfect timing.

When they both came again, this time she dropped on top of him, and he decided that they'd played in bed long enough. She'd fallen asleep again, and he got out of bed quietly so as not to disturb her. Going to the bathroom to shower, he felt better than he had in a very long time. He wondered if it was because he'd had the best sex of his life or that she had come to him again. Either way, he was whistling as he made his way down to Davy's room to see what he was up to.

Still asleep, too, he left them to their beds. There was no point in either one of them getting up, so he left them to it. Getting himself some breakfast of a bowl of cereal, he made his way to his office to figure out some more investments. Trevor had been keeping them all on the beneficial investments since he'd joined the family, and he couldn't be happier. As he finished up what he was doing, he heard Davy and Lisa coming down the stairs. It was nearly nine in the morning, and he had been up for about three hours.

Kissing Lisa on the lips, he kissed Davy on the head. They were ready for the day to begin, and he was glad that he was going to be there with them. As soon as they had their breakfast, he had a second one to join them, and they bundled up in their winter clothing and headed outside. Their driveway had already been done and was cleaned off of the nine inches of snow, but he wanted to make a snowman with his family, and that was what they set about doing.

At one-thirty, they were heading back to the house for lunch and some hot cocoa. It wasn't terribly cold out, but the snow was starting to come down again. He was glad it was Friday, as it was standing right now, they'd more than likely wouldn't have school again if it were any other day of the week. Gathering around the fireplace, they were happy to have it lit for them so that they could get warm. His cheeks were hurting; he'd been laughing so hard since they went out.

He had some work to do after lunch, and Lisa

had papers to grade. Davy was content to go to his room for a few hours and read his books. He loved to read and was glad that he'd been able to get him some books in his reading range the last time he'd been in town. The library had a lot of books for Davy, but since he didn't know what he'd read or not, he would just buy them and pass them on when he was finished with them. He was reading at a fifth-grade level according to his teacher, and he couldn't have been prouder of him.

Dinner was fast approaching when he finished up his work. Lisa had been done for a while and was playing a game with her son. As soon as he was able to join them, Davy was declared the victor, and they put that one away in favor of something else. Lisa had had a lot of such games at her house when she moved in with him, and he was happy that she had. It was fun playing games on a snowy day when they couldn't go anywhere.

Cassian walked over to his house about the time they were sitting down to dinner, and they invited him to join them. He said that he had some paperwork for him that couldn't wait, and he'd just go home. He'd only come over to bring him the work and didn't plan on staying.

"At least sit with us. You know it's been a long time since we've been able to have dinner together.

What with the weather and all." He said that he missed it too and couldn't wait for summer. "I know what you mean. I want it to be warm too out. My feet are always freezing."

As they were finishing up with dinner, Cassian did have to go. He said that Raven was holding dinner for him, and he didn't want to eat that late. When he left, they had their dessert and settled in the living room to watch some television.

"Just go and do whatever needs to be done." He asked Lisa what she meant. "You're not watching the program, so you might as well do what you want. Go do the job that he brought you so that you can quit worrying about it."

"I thought that I was hiding it well." She said that he might have someone else, but not her. "I'll only be as long as it takes me to get it taken care of. No working on things that can be put off until tomorrow. I promise."

"Just do what you need to do. I understand." Davy said that he understood, too, but he had a feeling that he didn't have any idea what they'd been talking about. The show was one of his favorites and he hated to miss it. "You'll even sleep better if you get it done rather than worrying about it all night."

As soon as he opened the file, he nearly went back to the living room to watch television. It was going to take him hours to sort out the stack of contracts that needed his attention right away. Two of them were due on Monday, so he had only had a few days in order to get them ready. The rest were due this coming week, so he had to work on those as well. He was going to be busy for the next several days before he got them finished, and wasn't looking forward to it. He wanted to spend time with his family, and he hated having interruptions when they were both home with him.

"I'm headed to bed." He looked at the clock and couldn't believe that it was nearly eleven o'clock. "You don't stay up too late, or you'll be exhausted again. There won't be any school, of course, but we still love having you around at breakfast."

"We'll have a big one tomorrow too since we all have the day off." He was determined to get the paperwork done before tomorrow and was going to work all night if he had to. He knew that he could nap during the day if need be, but spending time with his family was going to be a priority. He loved them very much.

It was nearly five in the morning when he finally finished with the first two contacts. He nearly started on the second ones, but decided that he needed to get to bed for at least a little while. Since he'd not gotten to sleep late this morning, he felt better than he had when he stayed up all night other times when he had to work late. It had only been about an hour, but he had needed it and wanted to get up with Lisa and Davy to have a big filling breakfast.

He was just barely able to get up, but since he didn't have to worry about the contracts anymore today, he felt like he could make it. Breakfast was just what he wanted, and when he asked for seconds on the hashbrowns, he knew he was going to have a good day. Davy was talking about going out into the snow again, and he was going with him to build a snowman again. The other was still out there, but Davy said that he needed a friend. So right after breakfast, they bundled up again and headed outside. The snow had finally stopped, but there was plenty enough for them to make several snowmen if they wanted.

"I know that I should have given you the contracts earlier in the week, but I was putting it off in favor of hanging out with Raven. She's doing so well in college that I find I want to help her out when she studies. Sometimes we don't get a lot done, but it's fun for the two of us." He told Cassian that it was fine, he had been able to get them finished up and would do the others this week. *"Good. I'm sorry about that. I'll be more productive when I have to bring you things to look over."*

"We're building a snowman, but if you need something, just tell me, and I'll go in and take care of it. I have the other contracts sorted out; I just have to go over

them to see if there are any flaws that are going to trip us up. Did you notice the one from the city? I thought they had their own attorney?" He said that Tank had asked for a second opinion on it. That something about it didn't ring right. *"Then we should advise them not to sign it. You tell him about gut feelings and not doing anything when your gut is telling you no?"*

"I tried to tell him, but he kept saying that he's more than likely wrong. It's one of the businesses that wants to come to town. Something about the tax abatement that they want is off." He said he'd look it over, but would recommend that they didn't sign it. *"I thought you'd say that too. I'm glad that we're on the same page on that. Also, there is one contract in the pile about the new nurse at the schools. They're only going to hire one and have her go to different schools every day. I don't know how that's going to work out. You know as well as I do that if she's at one school, something is going to happen at one of the others. And we'd be paying her a fortune in mileage."*

"Is this a trial thing or the way they're going to go with her?" He said the way the contract read to him was the way they were going to have her do things. *"That's not going to work. Aren't you on the school board?"*

He had to pause a moment to put the large ball they'd made on top of the other. He smiled at Lisa when she asked him if he was all right. Telling her that he was talking to his brother, she said that was good.

At least he didn't have to go out again. That was just too cold.

"Yes, I am, and so is Kaida. With you having a kid in the system, you should think about joining too. They can always use new people on it. Also, think of this about the nurse. If Davy is hurt, she's not going to be around to help him. I thought that I'd just throw that out there." He thanked him. *"No problem. I'm thinking that they need at least three nurses. One for each school would be optimum, but that would be running into some big bucks. I don't see the high school needing as many knees bandaged up, but you never know. Just give me your opinion on things, and I'll take it to the board. I just don't see how one is going to be doing the job."*

He didn't know if Cassian realized this or not, but he helped him with his work for the rest of the week. Now that he knew what he was looking for, it would be a simple matter of marking through the areas and returning them. He didn't think that one nurse was going to be doing a good job either, but then he wasn't in charge. Had he been, he would have had one for each school. The high school wouldn't need one there every day, he didn't think, but he did want to have one show up on occasion so that she could make sure records were up to date.

After closing the connection to his brother, he enjoyed the day more. His work inside was still calling to him, but he felt like he would make short work of it when he got around to getting to it. He did worry about the tax abatement, but like he told his brother, if it was off, then they would not sign it and wait for another business to come around. They had a lot of businesses calling them weekly to have a business put into their town.

When they went inside after getting the snowman built, they warmed up by the fireplace. The living room was fast becoming one of their favorite rooms because of the fireplace, and he'd recommend one to anyone who was thinking of building a house. It was the sudden warmth of the fire that he loved, and being able to get warm by it when you came in out of the cold.

After lunch, he decided that he needed about an hour-long nap. He told Lisa to not let him sleep any longer than two hours, as he wanted to hang out with the two of them more. Once he was on the couch, he fell asleep quickly and was surprised that he slept for the entire two hours. It seemed to him like he'd only just laid down, but he was rested again and was ready to tackle a good game with Davy.

The others decided that they wanted to get together for dinner and to watch a little bit of college football. He was up for that, but Davy wanted to stay home, and he didn't blame him. There was nothing for him to do there, and he didn't seem to care for football. Lisa decided to stay home too, so that she could get her paperwork caught up and be ready for tomorrow when the snow was supposed to be coming down more. This was not his favorite time of year. He much preferred the summer months to winter all year round.

Since the game they were watching was being played out west, it was nice to see the boys in t-shirts instead of long underwear on the sidelines. The game was a tight one in that both teams did their best. The winning score was 17-19, with their team scoring the most points. It had been fun and loud.

It wasn't until the game was over that he realized that the other women had gone to his house to hang out with Lisa. She told him that they showed up around halftime, and they'd been enjoying talking about the upcoming summer months.

"I told them where we were going for our Spring Break, and they're jealous. I told them that the park was big enough for all of us to go they should just make reservations and fly down with us. I think I about have them convinced. It would be epic to all be there at the same time, and it would give us someone to have dinner with nightly. They have some really good five-star restaurants there in the park." He asked her what the holdup was. *"They want to talk to their mates. I understand that. It's going to be a big expense for us, too. I'm glad it was easy for us to add you to ours so*

that you didn't have to get your own room."

"I'll talk to them now and see what they want to do. I'm assuming that they're going to want to talk to their wives, but that's all right, too. I can tell them what you've planned out and let them see how much fun it's going to be." She knew that he was going to say that, she told him, and was glad that they were going to be on the same page as each other. *"I can't believe how much fun we're going to have. I've never been to Florida, much less the park down there."*

As they were waiting for the next game to come on the television, they were eating the feast that had been laid out by the caterers. They ate a lot when they were together, and having it catered made it easier on the household that was hosting the events. He was glad that they fed him, he'd missed having a large lunch and was enjoying having a large dinner with his cousins. He told them about the park and when they were going, and they seemed like it was something that they wanted to do as well. Especially since Trevor was going with them, it would be more fun with his parents there, too.

~*~

Janice had only two weeks left to go on her sentence, then she was going to get out and make them all pay. She'd not been able to make anyone call Lisa, either, to have her bring David in to see her. Having a good memory, she was going to keep her list going until she got out of the stupid jail.

"Ninety days indeed." She should have been let out when they saw that she was an older woman. She could be the pitiful woman when it suited her, but they'd better not get used to her. She was only around when she needed things to go her way. "And they will as soon as I'm out of here."

She didn't know how it was going to work when she was finished with her sentence. It was bad enough that she had to be in this cell without her things around her. Her attorney, Max something, had better be getting on the ball with getting her out of here. He'd tried twice to get her a cell phone, but they checked his bags now, and he couldn't get past the guard with it. Damn it all to hell and back, it wasn't fair that she was in jail and Lisa was out and about causing trouble.

If she were honest with herself, she couldn't remember why she was in jail in the first place. Something about threatening Lisa and David, but she couldn't remember what it had been now. Or maybe she'd tried to kidnap her only grandson. He should have been with her all along and not with his mother, who was as stupid as they come when it came to raising children. Then there was something about a man.

"She's married, that's right. And wanting to adopt David. Well, I'll have the final say on that not happening." She tried to remember what else would have her in jail for three months, but it was all a bit fuzzy. All her days had run together since she'd been in here, and she couldn't for the life of her remember what the month was, much less the date. She knew the year, thank goodness, but the rest wasn't right there where she could remember. "That's all Lisa's fault, too. Her and that damned man that she's supposed to have been married to."

It didn't take her long to realize that she'd been married for sure. There was an article in the newspaper about how there was another Savage off the market. It had even featured a picture of the three of them on the front page about how they'd wanted a simple wedding at the courthouse. Janice was surprised that they didn't go all out, what with Lisa being able to spend as much money as she wished. The man would be broke within a year if she knew Lisa as well as she did. The damned girl was a twat and she hated her.

"Why?" Another thing that she couldn't understand about Lisa. She had a feeling that she'd never liked her. Janice knew that she'd married her son and that he'd been killed, but the details were like before, fuzzy. Something about his job or something along those lines. "For all I know, she might well have killed him, and I'd not remember it."

"Mrs. Manchester, your doctor is here to

see you." She asked who had set that up. "You did yesterday. You said that you were having memory problems and wanted him to see you. He's here now, or have you changed your mind about him again?"

"Again? He's been here before?" The twit nodded and didn't say anything more. "Well? Where is he? He's come all this way; bring me to him."

She had no idea how far he'd come because she didn't remember him at all. Much less want to see him. As soon as he came into the room with her, memories came pouring back to her about their last visit. She told him right off the bat that she couldn't remember the date.

"That's normal for being in jail. Your days will run together, and you won't remember the date because you don't have a newspaper or even a television to see. I just want to ask you some questions about your health, and we'll go from there." He asked her about a dozen questions, none of which she had an answer for. "You're doing fine, Janice. Just fine. Tell me what brought you into the jail in the first place. Surely you remember that."

"I can't. Something about Lisa and my grandson. She wants to take him away from me. Well, I'm going to be raising him even if I have to kill her to get to him. He should have been mine in the first place." He told her that she had to remain calm or they'd make him leave her. "I don't want to be calm. I want him with me so that I can raise him to be just like my David. Where does she get off marrying after my son died? She should have died with his name on her lips and not married some Savage person just because he has a lot of money. I have money, too, and I'm going to use it to get what I want."

"I'm afraid that I can't help you with that, Janice. You're going to need to calm yourself down before you have another heart attack. You don't want to end up in the hospital again, do you? The last time you were in there for nearly six months. I know how you enjoy your freedom. You might not be so lucky this time." She asked him what he was going on about. "You might not make it this time with the way that you're going. I suggest you calm down and let her raise her son. If you're this stressed out just getting him, what are you going to do with a kid in your house that isn't going to be happy with you for killing his mom to get him?"

"He'll not know. No one will tell him unless it's me. If they do, then there will be hell to pay, and I'm not afraid to use some of my considerable wealth to make sure that happens." He pulled something out of his bag and handed it to her. "What's this? Nitro? I have no need for anything like that. I'm as healthy as a horse."

"You're not, and I believe you know it. Right now you're rubbing your chest where your heart is supposed to be." She eyed him hard and asked him what he was talking about. "You're having chest pains right now if I don't miss my bet. You keep this up, and you're going to be dead before you get out of here. I want you to be on a better diet too. All this food that they're feeding you might be good to eat, but it's not good for you."

"Don't you be messing with my diet. I love what I'm getting to eat here. It's all I have to look forward to on a daily basis." He told her that she was going to die before she got out of jail again. "You leave my living to me. I know what I'm doing, and I'm going to be around a lot longer than you will be. Mark my words. If I don't have David by the end of the month, then I'm going to be going on a hunting spree that this little town will be talking about for generations. See that I don't."

"It's your funeral." He packed up his things and left the small vial of nitro pills on the table between them. "That is for you. Put one under your tongue and let it dissolve. If you need more than three, have them call an ambulance for you. I'm serious, Janice. You're going to be dead if you don't calm down and take care of yourself. And starting right now."

"I know what I'm doing." He nodded once and left her to her own devices. She didn't know what she was doing, and the pressure in her chest was so bad that she took one of the small pills and put it under her tongue. The pain lessened, but it didn't go away. She didn't want to die in the stupid jail, so she was going to pop them like candy until she was feeling better. By the time she took the second one, she was feeling better and decided that she was going to keep them on her if they worked that well. Not that she'd admit this to anyone, but she was sort of afraid of dying.

Chapter 10

Tank enjoyed being his dragon. It was something that he never thought he'd be able to do until recently. Now he'd spend his entire days just lazing around the yard as his dragon, and he didn't care who needed him. Expect that he knew he'd shift back to his other self if anyone were to need even the simplest of things from him. He couldn't leave his family stranded if they needed him.

"I have two questions for you." He told his brother that he was there for him. *"Good. I wanted to know what you've been able to find out about the school board. I know we talked about it, but I've lost my notes somewhere, and I don't have time to tear the house apart looking for them."*

"The school board is taking on new members. I think that Lisa is going to be on the team if she gets voted in. I have no idea why they'd not do that, but stranger things have happened. They're taking on four new members, so that with the five that they have now, it will still be an odd number. I think that's brilliant, by the way. What's your second question?" He said he'd answered it about Lisa wanting to join the board. *"I'm not sure she wants to do that. I think that she's joining it simply because she has a*

son going there and wants to be updated on things that are going on.

"Whatever it takes to get her on board, I'm happy with the outcome. She'll make a good person on the team because she can think outside the box all the time. And she's not one to rush in on her answers." He said that he loved those qualities about her. *"I do as well. She's brilliant but doesn't let it go to her head. I love her. When do you think we'll get our mates?"*

The question came out of nowhere, but he was used to that from his brother. He could jump around in conversations like that and had done it all his life. He said that he didn't know about finding a mate but was looking forward to it.

"I am as well. I don't know what sort of person she'll be, but I'm guessing she'll be just like the other women and not at all hiding behind me when there's trouble. I can see her being right out front of me and taking on the worst sort of people for me." He said that he could see that as well. A kick ass sort of woman. *"Yes, that's it. Kick ass. However, I won't be upset if she needs me on occasion. I need someone in my life other than you. I think we need to live in separate homes for a while."*

"I've been thinking the same thing. I know that we have the money now to do that, but I don't want to hurt the others' feelings by telling them that we're ready to move out on our own. Do you suppose they'll be all right with

that?" He said that he was sure that they would be. *"Yes, I guess you're right. They all have their homes now and seem to be happy. Not that they don't get together every time they're around."*

Tank thought about the last time they'd been together and how much fun he'd had. They'd get together when they could, and that was nearly weekly. He loved his cousins and was happy that they seemed to love him too. There was something so calming about them, even when they were arguing loudly about the refs on a game. Smiling, he thought of how he had won the last call that had been made and was happy for that. He didn't know a great deal about football, but he was learning.

After closing the connection with his brother, he decided that he'd had enough of the sun for one day. Shifting back into his other self was disappointing, but he knew that if he was going to get anything done, he was going to have to be his human self. People wouldn't be as happy to see him if he were his great dragon.

Heading into town, he was stopped by several people about the way things were going with the school board. He'd not realized it was such a big deal to have more members on the panel until then. As he was headed into the office where his brother was, he told him how he'd been stopped by so many people that he was surprised that they'd not increased the panel before now.

"Sometimes you just have to give a little push before things begin to happen, I guess. I've had several phone calls about that as well." They talked about the grants they were getting in the form of getting the sidewalks finished up, and he was glad that they'd looked into it. It was nice having things going their way for a change. "I heard from some Trail supporters. They're wondering what he's doing, not running against me in the next election. I simply hung up on them. I'm not going to get into that with anyone right now when things are going as well as we can make them. I have a date tonight. I met her online. I know you don't think that's such a good idea, but I'm sort of sick of seeing you across the table from me nightly. You're ugly if you want to know the truth."

"Gee, thanks. You know you're not as good-looking as you might think you are, either. I'd love to have a pretty woman sitting across from me, too." They both laughed, and he changed the subject again. He loved his brother, but wasn't going to be living with him forever. "I'm going house hunting in the morning. I need to have some space of my own."

"I understand that completely. I'll stay here since it's provided for me by the city, but I'd love to be able to find something that I can stretch out in on my own. Yesterday I spent nearly three hours as my dragon just chilling in the snow."

"I loved that I've been able to do the same thing. It's been great not having to worry about anyone freaking out about me being my other self." He thought about how they'd come to be dragons now when they'd not been before coming here. "I wish there was something that we could do for Lady Earth, but I'm sure she has everything that she's ever wanted. Having as much magic as she has, it's a small wonder that she doesn't have everything that she needs right at her fingertips. I don't know that I'd go that far, but I would make the town shine again if I could."

They talked about the contracts that Brenin had gone over for them. The next time they were meeting with the city council was in two weeks, and they were prepared. While Tank wasn't the mayor of their town like his brother was, he assisted him as much as he could. It was fun for him too. Just knowing that he was making a difference in people's lives every day was fun for him.

Tank went to his office in the big building and worked on some of the projects that he'd been putting off in favor of being at home. He didn't have a mate as yet, but he was going to be prepared when she came along. All he had to do was look out for her and be on his toes, and he'd be happy. Taking his cues from the others who had mates, he was happy to know that he was going to be happy with her when she came along.

After working on the paperwork for the new additions to the school board, he started looking for grants or low-interest loans he could get for the new stadium. It was in need of a complete overhaul, and he started looking for donors who wished to have their name on the field. The town would have to vote on it, of course, there would be a slight raise in taxes, but he didn't think they'd care all that much for having better seating at the games. They'd been able to get a new building put up for the concession stands, and he was quite proud of that. It was not only better, but it was bigger too. And with the donations that were coming in from some of the sponsors that were helping with it, he thought that they'd never have to purchase water bottles again for game nights. It would save them a great deal of money on that alone.

Usually, he didn't get involved with things like fundraisers, but there was one that was near to his heart. It was one for the grade school playground. He had a lot of fond memories of being by himself with Ace on the playground when he'd been a child and wanted the best for the kids.

There were all kinds of loans that he could apply for, and he decided that he was going to do just that. They'd have to build it themselves, but the money they'd save on having the materials purchased was going to go a long way in getting things done. He'd have the others helping him if no one else showed up. And with their extra strength, they'd have it built in no time at all.

It took him nearly four hours to get the application filled out. He had to keep going back over the instructions when it got to a new page. Tank wondered if many people got about halfway through the application and decided it was too much. But he was determined to get it done, and there wasn't any way that he was going to give up.

When he was finally finished, he printed off the paperwork and put it in the playground file with the other paperwork. It said that it would take six to eight weeks to hear back from them, so he wasn't worried about having enough time to get it put in before it could be used again. He figured that he'd hear from them about Thanksgiving and was looking forward to knowing that it was going to be taken care of.

After having lunch with his brother, he told him about the application for new playground equipment, and they worked on the things that were coming up in the following weeks. There were three luncheons that Ace needed to attend, as well as the meeting with the water board. They wanted to upgrade their system in reading meters, and they were both all for that. As it was now, someone had to walk to each of the houses to read the meters, and that was a long process.

Tank contacted one of the people that he'd been talking to about it and was getting information from him about getting things upgraded. It sounded just like something that they needed to invest in. The water company would be able to help with the costs, and that made it worth his while to get rolling on what needed to be done next.

They talked about the trip to Florida and decided they were going to go even if no one else in the family went. He had all the information from Lisa about what resort they were staying in, as well as the dates to go. Making the reservations right then, he was surprised to hear that others had done the same thing and gone ahead and booked their reservations too.

"Like I told the other Savages that have booked, we can get you all on the same floor, but we might not be able to get you rooms close together. That's the best we can do for right now. I hope you understand." He said he was just happy to be going and being on the same floor as the others. "Good. We'll do the best we can to accommodate you all together, but we're busy that week as there are a lot of schools out on Spring Break and wanting to come here to enjoy the lovely weather. I'm to understand that you guys have a lot of snow your way."

"Yes, we had about nine inches just the other day, and they're predicting more than that over the next week. I'm ready for summer." She said she'd never lived anywhere but Florida and didn't get snow where she lived. "That sounds heavenly. I would love warm weather all the time. My feet are freezing all the time."

After getting off the phone with the woman, he told Ace that they were booked. It was still far away yet, but it was something to look forward to when the time got closer. As soon as he was ready to call it for the day, Ace told him that he was ready to go home as well. They were still unpacking things that they'd gotten from the other house and were pitching out most of what had come to them. It was nice having a furnished house for work, but he couldn't wait until he had his own place.

Looking through the houses for sale in their area, Tank was able to find two that he thought would work. He set up a time to go and see them over the next couple of days and was surprised that the realtor was able to show them. She said that the roads would be cleared by then, and she was looking forward to working with him. He said that he was glad that he was going to be able to buy a house right now. After hanging up the phone, he felt good about what he was doing. Ace would be next in finding himself a house, and he was going to be there for him as well.

Now all he needed to do was find a mate, and he'd be set for life. He wondered how easy it was going to be and decided that he didn't care if it took forever. He was going to enjoy looking for her as much as he was finding her. She was going to be his everything.

~*~

Beth was bored. She had been sitting in the hospital room for the last two days watching her sister, and she wasn't entertaining her. Of course, she was dying, but that didn't mean that she had to sleep all the time.

"You know you can leave if you want. I didn't ask you to be here in the first place." She said she was her sister and wanted to be there for her. "No, you don't. I hear you mumbling about how much you hate being here. I can die with you here or not, Beth. It's not like you're going to be able to save me from anything."

"Well, aren't you just cheery. I want to be here, but it's taking so long." She knew that as soon as the words left her mouth, she shouldn't have said it. "I'm sorry that you're dying, but they told me that you'd only have six weeks to live. I had no idea they were going to keep giving you medication to keep you sleeping all the time. Why are they doing that in the first place?"

"I'm in a great deal of pain all the time. They're making me comfortable. Why don't you go out and get yourself something to eat? It's better than you taking pop shots at me because I'm taking too long to die." She said that she didn't say that. "You did. But that's all right. If it's all the same to you, I'd rather be alive than dead any day of the week. Just leave me to it and go out and have fun."

She thought about it for about five minutes and decided to do just that. After making sure that Helen didn't really care if she stayed, she left the room before she could change her mind. She didn't stop at the desk and tell them that she was leaving, as they had gotten testy with her when she'd asked them for something they were giving her sister for her backache. The chairs weren't all that comfortable, and she knew she was going to have to see someone about it before too much longer.

Putting her face up to the air to try and get the smell of death off of her, she reached into her bag to get her phone. Of course, it was Serenity again. And she'd not ask about her but their sister. She'd been the one who had stayed with their sister when things had been trouble for her work.

"I'm leaving now to get there." She said that she'd left Helen in her room so she could get something to eat. "You left her all alone? What sort of person does that to their sister, Beth? She's dying. There will be no second chances when she's gone. You should be asking her for her forgiveness instead of running off every chance you get."

"She told me to leave her alone." That wasn't quite right, but that's the story that she was sticking with. "Besides, you can sit with her for a few days. I'm sick of being cooped up in the room with her. It smells like dead people."

"That's because she's dying." She heard a car door slam, and there was someone else that Serenity was talking to. Something about the airport. "I'll be there in about two hours. If you're not there, I'm going to be pissed off at you."

"Be pissed. Helen said that I could go, and I did. She doesn't need me to hold her hand all the time. Half the time, she doesn't even know that I'm there. They keep her so doped up all the time, and she's sleeping it off." Now that her outing was ruined, she decided to treat herself to getting her nails done. It was something that she needed anyway, and no one was there to stop her. "I have things to do, so I'm not going to be there when you get there. Just know that I have a back pain from sitting around all day while you were out doing your thing."

"I was working." Rolling her eyes at her sister, she decided that she'd had enough. But Serenity apparently had more to say to her. "She's going to die, Beth, doesn't that mean anything to you?"

"She's been on the verge of death for the past six months. Either they find a cure for her, or they just leave her alone. It's boring sitting around the hospital room anyway." She knew that she was pissing her off, but didn't care. She'd been sitting with her for the past two days, and nothing had changed. "I might not even show up tomorrow either. You sit with our dying sister. I've had enough."

After closing the connection on the phone, she put her phone away, but not before muting it. It's not like she gave Helen cancer. It was just one of those things that had happened. Hell, she didn't even smoke. Hailing down a cab, she got in and asked the driver to take her to the mall. Surely, somewhere in there, she would be able to find a shop to do her nails for her. Maybe she'd get her hair done as well while she was at it.

Helen had been diagnosed with cancer about a year ago. After having chemotherapy, they said that she was cured. Well, not cured, but they'd done all they could for her. Then, about a month ago, she'd fallen, and they found that it was in her bloodstream and that it was too far gone for them to do much for her.

She had missed some of the conversation with the doctor when he'd been telling them about the cancer, but they only gave her five months to live. Beth had had no idea that it was going to be the full five months when she said she'd take her turn and sit with her. She'd also had no idea that it was just sitting with her while she had drugs pumped into her body, either.

Helen was talking to the woman who was doing her nails about her sister when she nearly took her finger off. She asked what she was doing when she saw the blood on her finger. There wasn't much of it, but enough that she thought they should give her the nail job for free now.

"How can you just sit here and act like it's an inconvenience to you that your sister is dying? Have you no heart at all?" She told her that it was none of her business what she did with her sister. "It wasn't until you told me about it. I mean, good Christ woman, she might only have hours to live, and here you are getting your nails done instead of being with her when she takes her last breath."

"You sound like my other sister. Serenity is forever going on about how we have a duty to Helen while she's still with us. I've not had anyone talk to me in a good long time, and I thought that you'd be sympathetic about my sister." She said the only one she was sympathetic with was her dying sister. "Figures. I'm always the bad guy when things like this come up. I didn't give her cancer. She just got it somehow. I wasn't going to stay with her at all if she could give it to me. I've seen what it would do to my body, and

I won't have myself taken away by some disease that makes you wish for death."

"Did she say that to you?" She said that she'd thought that if Helen had any lick of sense, she'd say the same thing. "You mean you'd rather she just die and get it over with instead of having you sit with her in her final hours?"

"Yes, that's it exactly. I'm not going to feel sorry for her either. Whatever she'd done to get herself in this way is entirely her fault." The woman told her to leave. "Leave? You're not even finished with cleaning my nails. I want a new set put on. And don't think I'm leaving you a tip either. I'm going to make sure that everyone knows how you nearly took my finger off, too."

"Get out of my sight. I want nothing to do with you anymore." She said she wasn't going to. "Yes, you are, or I'm going to call the police. I know my rights, and it says that if I don't want to deal with you, I don't have to give you service. So get out of here right now before I have you arrested. Surely there is something in the laws about being a cold, heartless bitch."

When the woman pulled out her cell phone and called the police, she left. No one else in the salon would finish her nails either. It wasn't her fault that Helen was dying, was it? She didn't give her cancer. People were just unfair about how they treated her, and she was going to have to figure out how to deal with them.

Pulling out her phone, she wasn't surprised to find that she had five missed calls from her sister. She didn't bother calling her back. She was free of the hospital, and she wasn't going to go back because Serenity was going to bully her. And she would too, she just knew it.

Finding someplace that would do her nails took her until nearly six. Promising herself she wasn't going to mention Helen, she found herself talking about herself. It was a better topic anyway, and she enjoyed talking about herself more than she did her sisters. They were both fuddy-duddies, and she hated to be around the two of them. As she was getting the final coat on her new nails, she thought again about having her hair done. But the thought of having to find someone this late in the evening didn't appeal to her. That was going to be something that she'd do tomorrow.

Finding her hotel after forgetting the name of the place she'd been staying since being in town, she went to her bathroom and took a much-needed shower. After washing her hair twice, just to get the smell out of it, she wrapped herself in the hotel robe and sat on the bed. Even if she didn't have anyone to talk to, this was so much better than sitting around the hospital room for hours on end.

It wasn't as if she stayed in her room for the two days she was watching over Helen. She'd made her way to the cafeteria looking for a good-looking doctor that she thought she could hook up with. Then, when that hadn't worked, she'd take walks around the building looking for something to do. Not only was Helen's room boring, but the entire hospital was as well. She didn't like to say this to her sister, but she might have to. If Serenity decided to die, she was going to tell her to do it on a cruise ship or something. At least she'd have something to entertain herself while watching over her.

When her hotel room phone rang, she decided to answer it with a cheery voice. It always made her feel better when someone commented on her voice when she answered that way. Waiting for the person on the other end to talk, she was ready to hang up when she realized that the person was crying.

"It's Serenity. Helen died an hour ago." Then the line went dead. Wanting to call her back, she pulled out her phone to give her a piece of her mind. Why had it taken her an hour to tell her? She was her sister, too, by god. Plus, she needed to make arrangements with someone to get her hair done now. There was no way that she was going to be looking like her dead sister when she could do something about it. "What do you want, Beth? I have to make arrangements for Helen."

"Why didn't you call me sooner so that I could be there with her?" she said that she'd left her messages. "I didn't get them. I had my phone on mute so that I'd not have to hear from you again."

"And just how do you think I was supposed to get in touch with you if you had your phone on mute? I'm not that good at tracking you down." She told her that she should have called the police to look for her. "My sister just died, pardon me for not calling the police to hunt down the one person who was supposed to be here with her when she died. I barely made it to the hospital to say my goodbyes. I'm guessing that you've had a wonderful evening with getting your nails done. Did you get your hair done as well? I'm sure you want to look good when we have her funeral."

"You're being really snippy. And yes, I got my nails done. They really needed it after being cooped up in that room for so long. Had I known she was going to die, I would have maybe stuck around longer." She told her that she wouldn't have because she was selfish. "I'm not selfish. I'm entitled. I know the difference."

"You make that sound like a good thing. But you're selfish too, if you want to know the truth of it." She made a sobbing sound, and it made her ask what was going on. "Helen just died, I told you. Would you like for me to be cheery with you? I'm not going to be, so don't even answer that."

"She's better off dead anyway. You told me that she was suffering. I never saw it. They were keeping her so doped up all the time, she barely acknowledged me when they came in to give her more meds. How was I supposed to know that she was going to die tonight?" Serenity didn't say anything, and that pissed her off, too. "We'll have to make the arrangements, I suppose. Another few hours of time that I'm never going to get back."

"You're such a bitch. How did I miss that for all the years that you were growing up?" She said she never paid attention to her. "And now that I do, I'm not at all happy that we're related. Helen had made her arrangements when she first got sick. All you have to do is show up and be there. You don't even have to watch over her anymore, either. She's gone."

When she hung up the phone on her end, Beth wanted to throw her phone across the room. But she didn't. The company said they'd not replace it anymore if she did that. Instead of putting it away, she looked at the messages from her sister.

"She doesn't have much longer to live."

"Get here if you want to see her again."

"You're not going to make it if you're not already in the hospital."

"She's gone, Beth. Our little sister is gone."

Before You Go...

HELP AN AUTHOR

write a review

THANK YOU!

Share your voice and help guide other readers to these wonderful books. Even if it's only a line or two, your reviews help readers discover the author's books so they can continue creating stories that you'll love. Log in to your favorite retailer and leave a review. Thank you.